Double Crossed

Paradise Cruises Series: Book 2

AE Moran

The Invisible Publishing Company

Contents

Chapter 1: Holly

"Welcome aboard Paradise Cruises!" a chipper young woman named Allie greets me.

I smile back at her. "Hi," I tell her. "I'm Holly Silverman and this is my husband Carlos. We need to check in."

She taps her stylus against the tablet in her hands and grins at both of us. "Yep. You're all set to go. You're in Cabin 58A. You can go on upstairs and settle in, but you need to be back down here in half an hour for the safety and security briefing and tour of the ship. Then you can kick back, relax, and enjoy your voyage."

She gives me one last big, beaming smile. I smile back at her and step around her to enter the *Electric Emerald's* main piazza. "

This is wonderful!" I walk over to the big windows looking out over the ocean. "I can't wait to see everything! Oh, look! There's the main concourse! Wow! It's like a little city all its own."

Carlos comes up behind me, slips his arm around my waist, and nuzzles into my ear. "You won't be seeing any of it if I have my way."

I laugh and pull out of his arms. "My fertile days don't start until day after tomorrow."

He doesn't back off. He draws me closer so he can circle my waist from the front this time. "There's no rule that says we can't do it before then. I'll still have just as many bullets then as I do now."

I blush. "Are you sure about that?"

"Absolutely sure." He leans in to kiss me. "This cruise is going to be the ticket. I hope you're ready to blow up like a balloon after this because you are not getting away from me this time."

I kiss him back. "If you're right, it means we'll have to take a cruise every time we want to have a child. We've been trying for eight months and nothing else has worked."

"Then this must be the secret." He plants one more kiss on my neck. "Let's go put our carry-on bags in the cabin and come back down here. You might not be able to walk if we start before the tour."

I blush and giggle again. He hasn't stopped talking like this ever since we booked this cruise.

He gives me that look again when we get into the elevator, but too many other passengers get in with us. He can't start anything here.

All this sex talk excites me, but it almost makes me nervous. Our busy schedules in everyday life interfere with us getting pregnant, not to mention the stress.

Now we have nothing else to do all day and all night. I hope he doesn't take offense if I want to explore the ship and maybe talk to a few people other than him. I don't want to stay locked up in our cabin for the whole cruise.

We exit on the top deck, find our cabin, and put our bags inside. I go out to the balcony and look out over the ocean again. "This is amazing!" I exclaim. "You can see everything up here!"

He comes up behind me and wraps his arms around my waist from behind. "We can watch the sunset from up here. That will be nice."

"Look at all those pools! And there are the lifeboats. Oh, look. They're starting the safety tour. We should go downstairs."

He lets me turn around, but he keeps his hold on me again. His dark, smoldering eyes go hard and intense when he stares deep into my soul.

"Don't think you're going to keep running out on me," he tells me. "You're all mine and I plan to make the most of it."

I feel my cheeks burning again. "You only keep reminding me of that every five minutes. Do you think I'm using the safety briefing to get away from you?"

"You might be."

I slide my arms around his neck and kiss him. I kiss him deeply and passionately to show him how much I want him.

He's the most magnetic, romantic, considerate man I've ever met and he's all mine.

That kiss builds faster than I expect. It turns into a rapid series of head movements and our breath quickens as he tightens his grip on me.

His body goes hard and my excitement takes over. He backs me into the cabin, pushes me against the wall, and pulls my shorts off before he starts pulling my thighs up around his waist.

I gasp and then cry out as he drives into me. He pants and husks in my face. I'm spiraling out of this world too fast on his cruel thrusts, but his passion and heat drive me wild. I can't stop.

He slams in harder and spikes me into a dizzy orgasm. I collapse on his shoulder as he roars in my ear and releases into me.

His voice dwindles to growls and groans. He pulls me off the wall still wrapped around him, collapses on the couch, and falls on top of me.

His mouth sinks against my neck and then crawls up to my ear. "Beautiful...." he whispers. "So beautiful....."

I drift into a daze of sex-drunk bliss. My rational brain knows we should go down to the piazza for the safety briefing, but I don't want to move.

He pulls away first and tries to lift off me. I hold on tighter and wrap my legs around him.

He bursts out laughing in my ear and sinks back down on top of me. "Do you plan to keep me tied up in here for the whole cruise?" he teases. "What if I want to get out and explore the ship?"

I let him go and collapse back on the couch. My body goes limp and I sprawl. "Tell Allie and whoever that I'm not feeling good. I'll have to miss the briefing."

"I won't tell them anything. Put your shorts on. Let's go. Then we can come back here and no one will ever interrupt us again."

I roll all the way onto my other side, put on my shorts, and spend just a few minutes cleaning myself up before we leave the cabin.

He laces his fingers through mine on our way down the hall. He grins at me and his eyes sparkle with so many suggestions and hidden meanings.

My heart skips a beat when we get back into the elevator. We're more in love than ever. I have the same good feeling about us getting pregnant on this cruise. This voyage is going to be the greatest experience of our lives.

We step out of the elevator onto the piazza, but we can hardly go anywhere. Dozens of people crowd the area to listen to the briefing. It's just starting.

"Hi, everybody, and welcome aboard your Paradise Cruise Line vessel *Electric Emerald*. My name is Allie Rosche. I'm the activity coordinator for the Electric Emerald." Allie gestures to a broad-shouldered, muscular, steamroller type guy standing next to her. "This is Troy Nixon. He's the Chief of Security for the ship. If you have any safety or security concerns, Troy is your man. His office is right down that hall, the third door on the left. His door is always open to you if any security issues arise. You'll also see him and the other cruise line security personnel around the ship keeping an eye on things and ensuring the safety of the ship, the crew, the staff, and the passengers."

Troy stands in silence through this whole speech. He wears an immaculately tailored navy blue suit that somehow perfectly matches his sandy brown hair.

His icy blue eyes never stop searching and studying the passengers in front of him. He isn't here to help Allie with the briefing and tour. He's here to evaluate all the passengers for any obvious red flags or inappropriate behavior.

No one does anything out of the ordinary—not right now. The cruise hasn't even started yet.

Carlos moves a little closer to me and puts his arm around me in a protective gesture. He's being a lot more physically demonstrative since we checked in on this cruise. He's usually too busy or distracted for stuff like that in our normal daily lives.

Allie goes on with the tour, leads us to different parts of the piazza, points out everything, and gives us a bunch of safety information about how to board the lifeboats in the unlikely event that we have to evacuate the ship.

She leads the way onto the rear deck and points up. "The bridge is up there. You can see the captain and bridge staff steering the ship and making all our course and navigation decisions up there. If in the event of an emergency you need to signal to stop the ship, you'll find these emergency stop buttons located in different parts of the ship and in each passenger suite. These buttons will bring the ship to an immediate stop, so only use the button in the event of a serious emergency such as a passenger falling overboard or something similar."

Carlos and I get caught in the crowd as she moves past the concourse and onto the main forward activity deck. She continues to show us around, but I find my attention wandering to the ocean beyond the ship's prow.

We'll be sailing out there any minute with nothing but open ocean in front of us and all around us.

We'll be sailing into an unknown future, but it will be just as beautiful as this smooth, flat, perfect ocean. Everything about my life is going to be perfect from now on.

Chapter 2: Nate

I slip my arms around my wife from behind and pull her against me while we stand on the forward deck.

The *Electric Emerald's* activity coordinator, Allie Rosche, gives us a rundown of the safety rules for the pools and age limits for the kids' areas.

The other passengers stand around listening. A bunch of couples hug each other the way I'm holding my wife, Alexis, right now.

Troy Nixon, the Chief of Security, doesn't bust anyone for getting romantic during the briefing. He doesn't pay any special attention to us or the other couples.

I don't pay much attention to the briefing. She feels too good in my arms.

I'm not the only person distracted by their significant other. Not many of the couples pay attention. That could be a problem if we have an emergency, but holding onto my wife like this feels a lot more important right now.

I lean forward to whisper in her ear. "We're going to do a lot more of this."

She giggles, but she does it silently so we don't disturb the briefing or the other passengers.

Allie moves on. She travels much more quickly through the ship showing us where we can find the golf course, the climbing wall, the weights gym, the massage studio, and all the other activities and features.

I slow my pace so the rest of the crowd passes us. I wind up dragging Alexis to the very back of the crowd.

I stay with the tour just long enough to hear it end and Allie wishes everyone a safe and happy voyage.

The crowd starts to break up and I tug Alexis around a corner. I sink back against the piazza wall and pull her against me so I can kiss her.

"Not here!" she whispers. "We have a suite for this."

"I can still kiss you in public. This is supposed to be a romantic tour. Come on. I never get to spend any time with you."

She blushes and leans into me even when she shoots me side looks. "Whose fault is that?"

"Yours," I tell her.

She laughs, pulls away, and pretends to swat me. "Very funny, Mister I-travel-all-the-time-for-work-and-can-never-make-it-home-to-see-my-wife."

"I told you I would downgrade to a local job whenever you want me to."

She draws even farther away, but she doesn't stop me from taking her hand so I go with her. "Don't start that whole discussion again. We're here to enjoy ourselves."

I follow her down the piazza toward the elevators. Is she leading me back to our suite? I hope so.

I wait until we get into the elevator before I ease up next to her. I want to radiate my desire into her so she feels it. "When do you want me to get a local job so I don't travel so much? You said you would tell me, but you never do."

"You keep saying you would have to take a reduction in pay," she reminds me.

"I would, but wouldn't it be worth it? We could start planning to have a family if I was coming home to you every night."

"But you said we would have to sell the house and buy something smaller. You wouldn't be able to afford our house on a local salary."

"So? Do you want me to come home or not?"

She looks away, and right then, the elevator opens on our deck. I keep holding her hand on our way back to our suite.

We've talked about all of this a million times before. She wants me to stop traveling for work, but she doesn't want to take the cut in lifestyle that would come with it.

She leads the way back into the suite and lets go of my hand so she can go out onto the balcony.

I wait a few minutes to give her some time before I follow her. She faces into the wind so the breeze blows her wavy blonde hair back from her face.

I cup her cheek and pull her in to kiss her. "We'll work it out one way or the other," I tell her. "We can get through anything."

Her features pinch with emotion and she fights her lips under control before she looks away from me. "I don't want to wait any longer," she chokes. "I want to start a family now."

"Then I'll take the local job."

"But I don't want to lose the house! I love that house! I don't want to live anywhere else."

"It's just a house. What house we live in doesn't matter, especially if we have a family. What matters is the family that lives *inside* the house and that starts with us—you and me."

She turns away to look out over the ocean. "We've already talked about this too many times."

"Then I just have to wait until you tell me you're ready to move—unless you want me to get all male and just make the decision for you."

She bursts out laughing and goes back inside the suite. "You wouldn't dare."

I follow her. "Why wouldn't I? What if I don't want to wait anymore, either? What would you do if I came home and transferred to a local job without telling you first? Then you would have no choice. We would have to sell the house, downgrade, and then you would have to deal with me being at home every night. What would you do then?"

She shoots me a smirk over my shoulder. "Is that supposed to be some kind of threat?"

I hold up both hands. "I really want to know. Do you think you could handle a man in your bed every night? You would never get any sleep."

She won't stop blushing and giggling at me. I grab her hand and pull her down onto my lap on the couch.

I have to kiss her like this. Her presence intoxicates me. I'm seriously considering making the decision for her.

I don't want to spend another day away from home. I want to come home to her every night and feel her wrapping herself around me just like this.

She sinks into my arms with a sigh. Her body responds when I caress up her ribs to her breasts and start peeling off her clothes.

She turns around to straddle me. Her voluptuous body undulates in front of me right where I can touch and stroke and play with everything.

Our bodies fit together perfectly. The rest is just logistics. She leans forward to kiss me as our rhythm picks up speed and power. She sits back smoking with fiery desire as she rocks and rides on top of me.

This is perfect. I think I will transfer to the local job no matter what she wants. I don't want to travel anymore after we get home from this cruise. I don't want to live away from her.

I finally lay her naked on the couch completely spent. I go to the bathroom and come out to hear my phone ringing in my pants pocket.

I get it out, but not quick enough to take the call.

Alexis snorts from the couch and pushes herself up into a sitting position. "Aren't you even going to turn your phone off here?" she snaps. "Are you really going to spend our entire cruise working on your phone?"

I hold the phone up so she can see the screen. "It's a phone call from my father. You don't mind if I stay in touch with family on this cruise, do you?"

"It wouldn't be the first time you interrupted our time together for work." She shoots to her feet and takes off around the room putting her clothes back on.

"What do you want from me?" I fire back. "How do you think I pay for that big, fancy house you love so much and keep you in this lavish lifestyle? Some of us have jobs."

"You don't have to spend all your time at work, Nate!" she snaps over her shoulder. "When you're with me, you need to be with me, not glued to your phone."

"I'm not glued to my phone. I have obligations and responsibilities, one of which is to provide for you. How do you think it's going to go when we have a family? If you can't handle it now, you won't be able to handle it then."

She doesn't turn around while she pulls her blouse over her head. "I don't want to argue about this anymore. We're here to have a good time. Just turn your phone off so I don't have to worry about it."

"I'm not going to turn my phone off, sweetheart. My mother is in the hospital having a cardiac procedure today. I told you all of this before. I'm going to keep in touch with my family to find out how she's doing and make sure my dad and my brothers are okay. You can't possibly have a problem with that."

She snorts again, goes into the bedroom, heaves her suitcase onto the bed, and starts unpacking it. She keeps her back to me the whole time.

I wait a few minutes for her to calm down. I text my dad and tell him we just checked in on the cruise line. He tells me my mom is out of the procedure and it went well. He and my brothers will wait at the hospital for the doctors to release her before my dad takes her home.

I tell him to keep me posted and I'll be in touch. He tells me not to interrupt my vacation. I tell him family is more important and I'll be staying in touch with them no matter what.

He thanks me and says my care means a lot to him and my mom. That's all I need to hear. So there. I knew I was doing the right thing.

I'm not prepared to budge on this, but I do have to make up with Alexis. I don't want our circumstances to mess up what's supposed to be a romantic cruise.

I go into the bedroom, sit down on the bed next to her suitcase, and take her hand. I have to hold onto her to stop her from walking away from me to put her stuff in the dresser drawers.

"Baby….I love you…." I tell her. "Let's just enjoy our time here. Let's not fight."

"I'm trying to," she counters. "That's what I'm trying to do."

"Then let's go downstairs and see what's happening on the concourse. There's too much to do here for us to dwell on our everyday problems. I'm sure they'll still be there waiting for us when we get back home."

I stand up and kiss her. She goes along with it and doesn't bring up all the sticking points we usually argue over.

I don't see any problem with downgrading our house. It's too big for what we need. It might even be too big for what we need to raise a family. Plenty of people raise families in less.

I don't tell her that, though. I've already told her in the past.

Sometimes I wonder if she would divorce me if I took a reduction in salary. Is our marriage really that fragile? Is that really why she stays with me?

Sometimes I have to wonder why she's so adamant about me staying at my current level of income. What other explanation is there?

Chapter 3: Holly

Carlos and I keep a hold on each other's hands when we step into the restaurant on the *Electric Emerald's* main concourse. A few other couples stand around waiting for the host to seat them.

One couple stands next to his podium while the woman yells in his ear.

He keeps pointing at the book in front of him and trying to explain something to her, but she won't let him get a word in edgewise.

"What's going on?" I ask the couple next to us.

"That couple was supposed to be part of a much larger party—that table over there." The woman of the couple points across the restaurant. Thirteen people sit around a circular table all eating, drinking, and enjoying themselves.

"Something went wrong with their reservation. Now these people can't sit with their friends." The woman makes a face at the lady doing all the yelling. "She sounds like a total Karen."

I find myself laughing. "Do you know this restaurant?" I ask. "Do you know if it's any good?"

"We don't know. This is our first time on one of these cruises. We didn't know where to eat, so Nate held up the list of restaurants, I shut my eyes, and pointed." She laughs. "That's how we decided where to eat tonight. It isn't scientifically proven or anything. It might be terrible."

I laugh along with her and hold out my hand. "I'm Holly Silverman. This is my husband Carlos."

She beams at me and shakes my hand. "Alexis Whitman. This is my husband Nate."

Nate and Carlos both turn inward to face us. All four of us shake hands and tell each other it's nice to meet each other.

Alexis is a tall, exquisite, bombshell with exaggerated curves and wavy, red-blonde hair. She reminds me of a much more worldly, savvy, Marilyn Monroe type 1950s knockout.

Her bright green eyes sparkle with girlish mischief. She looks like she has all the qualities to hold her husband's interest for a long, long time.

He's also tall—maybe an inch taller than she is. His hair is much darker and his dark brown eyes have a deep, thoughtful, almost Zen-like quality.

He strikes me as the kind of man who can be a rock for just about anyone. He's steady, reserved, and straightforward without being ostentatious about it.

"This place is packed," he remarks. "We should get one table. How about you two join us for dinner? We'll probably get seated sooner—and we'll have someone to talk to other than each other."

Alexis laughs, blushes, and leans into him when he puts his arm around her. They look happy together.

"That sounds great," Carlos tells him. "Did you talk to the host yet?"

"I'll do it." Nate walks over to the host's podium.

His size and immovable aura produce an instant effect on the irate lady standing there. He plants himself in front of the podium until the host turns to him instead.

The woman has to stop talking while Nate holds a conversation with the host.

"He put the fear of God into her," Carlos remarks.

"She better step off," Alexis points out. "It isn't like the restaurant doesn't have other tables. She and her husband could have gotten seated and served by now if she didn't cause such a stink."

Nate comes back. "He has a table for four already open. He doesn't have any for two, so we're in luck. Come on."

He leads the way and the host escorts us to a table on the opposite side of the room from the enormous party.

It's much quieter here. "Have you ever been on a cruise before?" Alexis asks me when we sit down.

"Nope. This is my first time. Have you?"

She grins at me. "No! Isn't it exciting? I watched the ship pull away from the pier earlier. It was like launching into space or something."

I laugh. "It is kinda like that, isn't it? At least we have plenty of food."

"And oxygen," she adds and makes me laugh again. "Where are you and Carlos from?"

"Spokane, Washington," I tell her. "How about you?"

"Hey! We're from Seattle!" She squeezes my arm. "Small world, huh?"

"Yeah. I'm an accountant, but I work from home. What do you do?"

She smirks at me. "I'm a stay-at-home trophy wife." She laughs. "If you see what I mean."

I definitely see what she means, but I don't say that. Nate must be doing pretty well for himself if he can keep such a stunning woman happy.

I have to change the subject, so I ask, "So what does Nate do?"

"He's a traveling sales rep for the Rush Network—but we've been planning for him to stop traveling and take a local position so we can spend more time together and start a family. That's why we came on this cruise—so we can spend more time together."

"Really? We're trying to start a family, too."

She reads my mind and her eyes drill into me. "What do you mean—you're *trying* to start a family?"

I turn bright red and look away. "I mean just that. We're trying."

She lowers her voice and all her mirth dies. "That sucks. I'm sorry."

I shrug it away. "Carlos works a lot, too. He's a hospital administrator, so the stress gets to be a lot for both of us. We're hoping this cruise makes it happen."

She smiles much more warmly. "I really hope it works out for you."

I find myself smiling back at her. "Thanks. I'm sure things will work out for you, too."

We both turn to listen to the men's conversation. They're both talking about their work. Nate and Alexis live in a swanky part of Seattle. He really must be doing well if he can afford to live there on only one salary.

Nate and Carlos talk back and forth for a while before it comes out that all four of us want families. Nate has three brothers. They're all married with children. He and Alexis are the only members of their family who don't have them yet.

Carlos also talks about his siblings and their families. I'm just trying to decide what to talk to Alexis about when she turns to me and asks, "So what do you do when you aren't accounting at home?"

I find myself laughing. "I'm a fashion blogger. I love your outfit, by the way. Your style is so impressive."

She blushes. "Thank you so much! I'm a sucker for the classics."

"Me, too. I wish I had your body to pull it off. Did you ever do any modeling?"

She turns bright red and waves that away. "Stop it. I could never do anything like that."

"Would you like to? I know a few photographers who are always looking for models. They pay, too."

Her head shoots up. "Really?"

"Of course. Women like you are hard to come by."

Her eyes dart to Nate, but he's too preoccupied with his conversation with Carlos. "I don't know about that....." she murmurs.

"I'm sure he wouldn't mind. I'm sure he's proud of you."

She doesn't get a chance to answer before the waiter comes. We all order. I don't restart the subject after he leaves. I don't want to make Alexis uncomfortable by bringing it up again.

"How did you get into fashion?" she asks.

"I studied it in college. I wanted to become a designer."

"Why didn't you?" she asks. "Passion like that is the foundation of a fulfilling career."

"I'm more of an observer, not a participant. My thing is evaluating the combination of colors, textures, and interplay of an outfit. I didn't want to spend my time sewing and fiddling with certain outfits. I get to see and appreciate dozens of outfits without staying on one particular one. That's the designer's job."

She nods. "That makes sense."

Right then, Carlos turns to Alexis and says, "Are you from Seattle originally?"

She starts talking to him about how she grew up in the Midwest. That's my cue. I turn to Nate.

"Carlos tells me you're an accountant," he begins.

"It's not the most exciting career, I know."

"Did I just hear you talking to Alexis about fashion?"

I shrug. "It's just a hobby I do on the side. I write blog posts about certain designs and trends in the industry, but I don't do it seriously. I could never do it as a job."

"So what made you go into accounting? It must have been a pretty compelling reason if you've stuck with it for so long. Other people might not find it exciting, but you must at least find it interesting."

I cock my head to study him. He stares back into my eyes with the same steady, level-headed, solidity I noticed earlier.

He's the first person who has ever asked me this question. Not even Carlos asked me why I chose to become an accountant instead of a fashion designer or a fashion commentator.

"I guess......it's like chess, you know?" The words rush out of me once I start talking. "I move the numbers around on the chessboard to make them do certain things. The numbers represent political intrigue, power struggles, personalities at work, and all the unlimited possibilities that go along with them. The numbers can fit together in an infinite variety of combinations, but the pattern they do fit into tells a story—a very interesting story. The story could be that the company is failing—or that someone is embezzling money—or that someone in leadership is incompetent and not managing the company right—or that the employees are on the verge of revolt—or that the founder is bored and wants to move on....There's always a story behind it and the numbers reveal that story. No one can cover it up. It's like a mystery I have to solve and maneuver the chess pieces into the right positions to win the game." I try to look away, but his steadfast gaze won't let me.

"That's the way I see it, at least. Other people might not, but I do find it interesting. It's actually far more interesting than fashion."

"That's fascinating," he murmurs. "I never thought of it like that, but you're absolutely right."

"What about you? Alexis says you're a sales rep. Do you enjoy that?"

"I enjoy everything about it except the travel. I mean, I like the travel, too. I just don't like staying away from Alexis so much—but I love everything else about it."

"What do you love about it? It probably isn't the kind of job most people say they would love."

He laughs. His whole face brightens when he laughs. He looks much softer, but no less Zen-like and rooted.

He reminds me of a kind of Buddha when he laughs even though he's broad-shouldered and muscular under his suit. He laughs from the roots of the Earth. That laughter sounds like it comes from the deep bedrock of his unwavering being.

"I suppose I see it like chess, too," he replies. "All the stories you just mentioned—they're going on all the time in the business world—and I'm one of the pieces. I'm the forward pawn that penetrates the enemy's territory. I interact and negotiate with enemy pieces and friendly pieces to maneuver our side into the best position."

"Are they actually enemies?"

"No, no. Not like that. They're just on the other side of the board. The game is to maneuver our side into a position where we win, but most of the time, that requires me to maneuver their side into a position where they win, too. So we both win. That's the game."

"Do you really see yourself as a pawn? Not a knight or a bishop?"

He blushes at me and his eyes twinkle. He looks so unbelievably happy, but not because of anything I said or did. He's happy in himself. He doesn't look like anything can shake him.

I know that isn't true. He's just a guy, but I've never met anyone like him before. I can see why Alexis appreciates him.

"Now you're trying to flatter me," he tells me. "I'm not a knight or a bishop. Besides, if you know anything about chess, you know that a pawn that makes it all the way across the board gets the power of a queen. He becomes the most powerful piece on the board—or one of them. That's me—or that's the way I see myself. I stay humble and do the job no one else wants to do, but that puts me in a position of being able to accomplish more than anyone else."

"Do you think you'll always do sales?"

"Not likely. We're talking about me taking a job at home so Alexis and I can start a family."

"She mentioned that. So how will you play chess then?"

He laughs again and his cheeks color. "I like talking to you."

My head shoots up. "Huh?"

"No one ever talks to me like this. I like where this conversation is going."

"Where is it going?" I ask.

"I just mean I like talking to you. It's fun to explore these ideas. I don't get to talk to other people like this."

I look away, but I can already see in his expression that he doesn't mean anything by it. He just genuinely enjoys the exchange of ideas.

"So?" I ask again. "What will happen when you change jobs?"

He shrugs. "I'm sure something will happen. I'm sure I'll find something interesting to like about it. I'm usually interested in everything, so I don't think I could do a job without finding something that I liked. Besides, I might take another sales job. I would be doing the same thing, just in the local area instead of traveling."

I nod, but the waiter comes with our food right then. The conversation doesn't restart until after he leaves.

Then I wind up talking to Alexis while Nate and Carlos talk to each other. I don't get a chance to talk to Nate again for the rest of the evening until we say good night and go off to our own cabins.

Chapter 4: Holly

Carlos and I hold hands as we stroll down the concourse. "Do we need to buy anything?" I ask.

He laughs. "I think we have everything we need. We don't need to buy anything."

"Do we *want* to buy anything?" I ask. "I feel like we should be spending money out here."

"Spend all the money you want, baby. Buy anything you want. I want to spoil you."

I laugh and glance around at all the stores. "I can't think of anything I want."

"What about jewelry?" He leads me to a jewelry store full of diamonds, gold chains, and rings in the window.

I pull him away from the display. "No way! That stuff is way too expensive!'

"Nothing is too expensive for you." He points to a diamond pendant. "I like that one—or those earrings. I could take you out to a fancy restaurant tonight and you could wear them."

I turn bright red and pull him away. "Stop it. I don't need any jewelry."

We continue strolling down the concourse until he gets a reminder on his phone. "That class I want to take is starting upstairs at the climbing wall. I'll meet you back at the suite later, okay?"

"Okay." I stop there while he kisses me goodbye. "Have a good time."

"Stay out of trouble." He lets his fingers trail out of my hand and hurries away to the elevator.

I wave goodbye and keep walking. I don't know where to go or what to do, so I decide to just explore the ship.

I head for the piazza when I see Nate entering the concourse from outside. "Hey, there. It's my favorite enemy pawn." He flexes his knees and holds up both hands in a martial arts pose. "En garde!"

I laugh at him. "That's fencing, silly."

He straightens up and saunters the rest of the way toward me. "What do you say when you want to attack someone with karate?"

"That wasn't karate, either, but if you really want to know, you say, 'Hajime'. It means, 'begin' in Japanese. That's what they say when you start a martial arts match."

He cocks his head to one side. "Really? How do you know so much about it?"

I shrug. "I'm a nerd that way. It's kind of like the referee saying, 'Let's go to war,' before a UFC fight."

He howls with laughter. "Oh, my God! I can't believe you're actually talking about the UFC!"

"Why? It isn't a secret."

He won't stop laughing. His cheeks flush and his eyes sparkle. "I can see I'm going to learn a lot from you." He nods behind me. "Where are you going?"

"Nowhere. Carlos just went upstairs for a rock climbing class. Where's Alexis?"

"She went to get a manicure and a massage. It's hard work being as stunning as she is."

"I'm sure it is," I mutter under my breath.

We both turn back into the concourse and start walking next to each other for no apparent reason.

"You and Carlos should come out to dinner with us again tonight," he tells me. "Unless you have some other plans."

"No, we don't have any other plans."

Nate smirks at me on the side. "I wouldn't want to interfere with your fertility efforts."

I snort. "You won't be. Trust me. We do stop for a few minutes at mealtimes."

He laughs again. "Thank God. I was starting to get worried about your physical health."

"Does Alexis have any outside interests? I didn't get a chance to ask last night. Oh, what am I saying? I didn't get a chance to ask you last night, either. Do you have any outside interests—or are you too busy traveling for work?"

"It's interesting that you mentioned chess in relation to your accounting work," he replies. "I actually study advanced mathematics while I travel."

I stop in my tracks and spin around to stare at him. "No, you don't."

He blushes again. "Don't tell anyone. It's a secret."

"Why is it a secret? Are you working for the CIA or something?"

"No, but I am learning coding at the same time. Math and coding. Those are my interests. I study them during long waits at the airport and in the down times between business meetings when I have nothing else to do. It's like learning another language—or, like we were talking about last night, more like learning the territory of a foreign country. I like it. It's interesting."

I start walking again. "That's sounds incredible."

"What about Carlos?" he asks. "Does he have any outside interests?"

"He exercises a lot. He changes up his workouts all the time so he's always doing something different."

"I exercise a lot, too. Exercise is *not* an outside interest. I mean does he have anything he does outside of work that he's interested in—something he's passionate about or learning about or something like that."

I find myself stopping and looking up at the ceiling. "I really don't know. That's strange, isn't it? Anyway, he's really busy and stressed out with work, so I don't think he has time for anything like that. You'll have to ask him. *I'll* have to ask him. I'll be interested to hear what he has to say."

He opens his mouth to say something, but his phone rings right then. He pulls it out of his pants pocket and checks the screen.

"I'm really sorry, but I have to take this. My mom had a cardiac procedure yesterday and my brother is calling me. I'm sorry."

"Don't be. I'll see you tonight. I hope your mom is okay."

"Thanks." He turns away and walks off extra fast holding the phone to his ear.

I watch him go. He's such a great guy—so easy to talk to and so down-to-earth.

I turn away and head off to the other end of the concourse. I still don't have anything to do. I suppose I could go get myself a manicure and a massage, too. That would be nice.

I turn around to retrace my steps. The massage studio is four decks above me. I have to take the elevator to get there, but I have plenty of time before Carlos finishes his class.

I'm just passing a Chinese eatery on my left when I happen to glance down the hall between the eatery and the movie theater next door to it. The hall leads to the eatery's kitchen.

I freeze to the spot when I see Carlos through an open door at the end of that hall. It leads into what looks like a greasy, grungy storage room packed with the eatery employee's uniforms, mops, kitchen towels, and a bunch of other restaurant supplies.

Carlos stands in front of a stainless steel worktable. Alexis sits on it in front of him with her knees drawn all the way up to her shoulders and her skirt hitched up to her waist.

She leans back on her arms while he plows between her legs. He manhandles her breasts through the front of her top and grabs her ass with his other hand to pull her into his thrusts.

I stare in sickening horror when I realize what they're doing. He bends all the way over and presses his face against hers, but they don't kiss. They're both panting and snarling in each other's faces too fast.

They bare their teeth in animal fury while he bumps her ass backward on the table. She widens her thighs to welcome him in. They're really doing it on the table in that restaurant storeroom.

Her cries escalate to screams until he turns his head to see where the door is. He doesn't turn around enough to see me watching from the concourse.

He tears his hand away from her breast just long enough to throw the door shut. It cuts off my view of them, but the door doesn't completely muffle the sound.

She starts screaming louder. I can still hear her very faintly from here.

I feel sick. I can't move, but right then, someone bumps into me. A guy turns around and says, "Oh, sorry!" before he walks off.

That moment snaps me back to my senses I take off walking fast. What am I going to do about this? What *can* I do about this? My husband is cheating on me—with Alexis.

How did this happen? They never met before last night. Are they really having such a raunchy hookup in the back room of some Chinese greasy spoon on a cruise ship?

I race out of the concourse heading I don't know where. I'm not watching where I'm going. I only know I have to get out of here.

I turn toward the elevators. I should go outside. I need to pace up and down so I can clear my head enough to think.

I round the corner too fast and run full force into a solid wall of granite. I bounce off before a man catches me by the arms. "Hey! What's going on?" he demands.

I struggle against that hold. I think at first that it must be Troy Nixon, the husky security chief, but it isn't. It's Nate.

I flounder in confusion. "I just saw them!" I blurt out. "I just saw them!"

"Hey!" he tells me. "What's wrong? What happened? Are you okay?"

"Nate....." I look up at him and the truth comes crashing down on top of my head. Tears spring to my eyes, but I can't stop staring around in wild panic.

Carlos....he was doing it....with Alexis. Nate will be crushed when he finds out—but I have to tell him I can't keep this from him.

"I just saw them, Nate!" I hear my voice rising out of control. "I just saw them!"

"Who?" he asks. His brow furrows in concern. He's more worried about me. He has no idea his world is about to come to an end. "You just saw who? Hey! What's wrong? You were fine a few minutes ago."

"I just saw them, Nate! Carlos.....and Alexis......they were doing it....."

He stares at me in stunned silence. He doesn't react at all.

"I'm telling the truth!" Tears streak down my cheeks, but I'm too out of my mind even to feel anything but alarm. "They were....in the storeroom.....behind the Chinese restaurant....."

His features turn to granite. He doesn't look like a happy, smiling, laughing Buddha now.

He grabs my elbow and turns me toward the concourse. "Show me!" he snaps. "Show me where they are!"

He marches me back onto the concourse. I'm too dazed to argue.

He storms to the Chinese restaurant and I stop outside the hallway. I don't dare to go down there.

I point. "They were down there....on that table......"

The door stands open. The room is empty except for all the mops and uniforms and supplies. Carlos and Alexis aren't in there anymore.

"I'm sorry, Nate!" I blurt out. "I had to tell you!"

He turns around still scowling and fuming in rage. He looks scary like this. "Thank you for telling me. I should have known something like this was going on."

"What am I going to do?" I flounder every which way in a panic. "What *can* I do?"

He takes my arm much more gently this time. "Come on," he murmurs. "There's nothing to see here."

He guides me to the elevator and we get into it. I can't stop squirming in every direction.

This revelation eats me up from the inside. I don't know how to contain it or cope with it. I can't even understand what's happening to me.

The elevator opens on the top deck. Nate escorts me back to the door to my suite.

"Are you going to be okay?" He shoots me a look. "Don't answer that."

"I....I don't....I don't know what to do....."

"It's going to be okay." He takes a step forward and rubs his hands up and down both my arms. "I'm going back to my suite to confront Alexis. I suggest you do the same thing with Carlos. We'll meet back up tomorrow and compare notes. Okay? Here. Take my number. You can call me if you need anything."

He takes a business card out of his pocket, scribbles something on it in pen, and hands it over.

He's written a phone number on the back of the card. This number is different from the business phone number on the front of the card. This must be his personal phone number.

I pass my hand across my forehead. I should thank him. "I'm so sorry...." I choke. "I never meant it to hurt you....."

"You didn't do anything to me," he mutters. "You did me a huge favor and I'm grateful. You deal with Carlos. I'm right down the hall if you need anything. Understand? Don't hesitate."

I nod, but I can't think straight.

He pats my arm one more time and walks off in the other direction. Now I have to deal with my lying, cheating, snake of a husband.

Chapter 5: Nate

I stalk back to the suite I share with Alexis. I only hope and pray Holly made a mistake about seeing Carlos and Alexis doing it in that restaurant storeroom.

My gut tells me Holly didn't make a mistake about that. She wouldn't have picked out that specific place unless she really did see them there.

She's even more distraught about this than I am. She didn't make it up.

Now I have to deal with Alexis. Just don't ask me how I'm going to do that.

I enter the suite and pace up and down. I can't sit still. If she did this now, what is there to stop her from doing it at any other time?

This can't be the first time. She only met Carlos for the first time last night. Both of them must have been moving fast. That kind of thing takes practice.

I could understand and believe it of him, but Alexis and I are supposed to be on a romantic getaway to spend more time with each other.

She lied about getting a manicure so she could hook up with a guy she doesn't even know. He was supposed to be at a rock climbing class, which means he lied to Holly, too.

This is the behavior of hard-core, experienced cheaters. This wasn't a one-time mistake.

Has she been cheating on me while I've been out of town on business? How would I find out? She must have left a trail of evidence.

It's a good thing she doesn't come back while I'm so steamed. She doesn't come back for another hour.

My mind immediately switches to all kinds of filthy thoughts about her doing it with another man. Is she standing there with another man's wetness in her panties right now?

He must have had his hands all over her. I'll never be able to touch her again. It's over.

She no longer looks beautiful to me. She looks like a low, cheap streetwalker cruising for her next trick. What the hell did I ever see in her?

Holly is so much plainer, but she's still beautiful in a humble, understated way. She has a trim, long, slender body. She isn't stacked to the limit like Alexis is and Holly doesn't flaunt it, either.

I used to love that about Alexis. I used to be so proud of how ostentatiously gorgeous she is—and she knows it, too. She knows every guy in the room wants her.

Now the sight of her makes me sick.

She smiles at me when she walks through the door. Her smile looks predatory and disgusting.

"Have you been here all this time?" she asks.

"No, I went down to the concourse and ran into Holly from last night."

She crosses the room to put her purse on the table. "That's nice. They're a nice couple."

"I talked to her for a while and then I had to leave to take a phone call from my brother. I went back over to the concourse afterward. I ran into her and she told me she saw you and Carlos hooking up in the storeroom behind the Chinese restaurant. Is that true?"

My chest hurts by the time I get it all out. I can't breathe. The next few minutes will decide my whole life.

She spins around. "You don't actually believe that, do you? How can you accuse me of that?"

"I asked you a question, Alexis," I snap. "I asked you if it's true that you hooked up with Carlos today. Just give me a simple yes or no or I'll know you're trying to hide it."

"Of course I didn't hook up with Carlos today!" she counters. "That's ridiculous! I only met the guy last night! You didn't see me, did you? Only Holly says she saw me."

"No, I didn't see. She took me back to where she says she saw you, but no one was in that storeroom then."

"There you go. She must have made a mistake. Maybe she saw Carlos hooking up with someone else and mistook the person for me."

"Have you spoken to Carlos at all—either in person, by phone, text, or in any other way since we had dinner last night? Tell the truth."

"Of course I haven't! Do you really think I'm in the habit of texting and calling other women's husbands so we can hook up in restaurant supply rooms? That's outrageous!"

I shrug. "You might be."

She narrows her eyes at me. "We're supposed to be here getting closer to each other, but we won't be doing anything with each other if you throw around accusations like that. I strongly suggest you double-check if Holly made a mistake. I'll be waiting patiently to hear your complete and unconditional apology."

She storms into the bedroom and slams the door in my face. I go into the other bedroom and shut the door behind me.

We haven't used this room. We don't need it—or rather, we didn't need it until now.

No way will I go back into the same room with Alexis after this. She's right that I need some more conclusive proof than just Holly's word, but my gut tells me I'll find it.

Holly was telling the truth. She didn't make a mistake. Carlos and Alexis really were doing it.

I spend an agitated night not getting much sleep. I actually start to doubt myself. What if Alexis is telling the truth and Carlos hooked up with someone else?

I wait in the other room so I don't have to see her. She leaves to go off somewhere. Maybe she's out there hooking up with someone else. How the hell should I know?

I'm going crazy and I can't think straight. I leave and realize I should have at least found out where she was going so I could avoid her.

This is what I've come to. I'm avoiding my own wife.

I head down to the concourse. I don't know where to find Holly to check with her about Carlos's reaction.

I find her on the rear deck above the ship's wake. "Are you okay?" I ask. "What did Carlos say?"

"He denied everything. I can't believe he actually had the nerve to bald-faced lie to me like that!"

"Are you one hundred percent certain you recognized who you saw? I believe you saw someone, but are you absolutely certain it was those two? You didn't make a mistake?"

She turns away and presses her hand to her forehead while she paces. "I saw both of them plainly, but I really started to question my own sanity when he said he didn't do it. What if I did make a mistake? What if....I mean....how could I not recognize my own husband?"

I study her for a second. Every ounce of my being tells me this woman is genuine. If she did make a mistake, it was an honest one. She didn't just wake up in the morning and decide to accuse her husband of cheating.

"Did you see anything...." I ask. "Any.....you know....any distinguishing characteristics....on Alexis, I mean? Anything in particular that you could use to identify her....like a birthmark or something?"

Holly frowns. "Well, she did have a scar on her knee—right here."

She draws a line from below her kneecap up along the side of her knee to the top.

I turn away and stare over the side. So it was her. Alexis was wearing a skirt below her knees at dinner that night. No way could Holly make that up.

She comes over to me and rests her hand on my shoulder. "I'm so sorry you're going through this."

"I told you not to apologize to me," I mumble over my shoulder. "You're the one good thing in all of this. At least I know I can talk to someone I trust."

"What are we going to do? Carlos won't budge. He insists there must be some misunderstanding and he loves me and all that. I even followed him after he left the suite. He didn't do anything. He just went to the gym and did his workout."

"We need proof. That's all there is to it."

"Where do we get that? There is no proof. I'm the only person who saw them."

"I have an idea." I turn around and face her. "Come on. We're going to get to the bottom of this."

Chapter 6: Holly

I follow Nate down the hall. He turns off into the ship's security office. We meet one of the security guards in the front office.

All the security guards wear dark, tailored suits, expensive leather shoes, and coiled earphones in their ears. They look like the Secret Service.

This guy wears a nametag that reads, *Beau Towers.*

"Can I help you?" he asks.

"We want to see Troy Nixon," Nate tells him.

"He's in his office. Give me a minute and I'll tell him you're here."

Beau heads into the back and leaves me and Nate alone.

"Are you sure about this?" I whisper. "It isn't like Carlos and Alexis are endangering the ship or anything."

"How else do you suggest we find out whether they really did it or not? They both know we're suspicious and watching them. They'll expect us to follow them. They would probably even expect us to work together so you follow Alexis and I follow Carlos. We need to get to the truth some other way."

Beau comes back. "He says for you to go right in."

He gestures for us to go down a different hall. Offices and rooms line both sides. One of the rooms is a giant control room packed with screens showing security footage from all over the ship.

Four guards work in there monitoring everything from the casinos and restaurants to the pool and all the hallways leading to all the suites and cabins.

The ship's security team even has cameras on the bridge and in all the staff and crew locker rooms and workspaces.

We find Troy in a much larger office at the end of the hall. He stands up to shake hands with both of us. "What can I do for you?" he asks.

"Holly here spotted her husband hooking up with my wife yesterday," Nate blurts out. "We confronted them both and they both deny it. We were wondering if there is any way you can give us proof—like security camera footage of the location where she saw them. I don't know if that's against your policies or anything, but we need some way to prove that it really happened. It would mean a lot to us if you could at least put our minds at rest about what actually went down. We're going crazy as it is."

He nods. "Yeah, I can do that. Everyone who came on board signed a waiver agreeing to the ship's security policies, which include camera surveillance of the ship for security reasons. Follow me. We'll see if we can find it."

He walks around his desk and reenters the hall. Nate and I exchange glances on our way back to the control room.

Troy gets on one of the computer stations and sits down in the swivel chair. "Where did you see them? If it's anywhere in a public space, we should have footage of them."

"I'm not sure if it's a public space or not," I tell him. "They were in the supply room behind the Chinese restaurant. I was on the concourse and I saw them down the hall."

"What time was it?" Troy asks.

"Um.....I'm not sure, exactly. I guess it would have been sometime between ten and eleven in the morning."

He navigates through a bunch of different feeds and pulls up footage from the concourse at the ten o'clock mark. He locates me and Carlos walking around and him looking into a jewelry window.

Troy uses the computer to track our movements to the spot where Carlos left to attend the rock climbing class that never happened.

Then Troy uses the same combination of maneuvers to follow me until I meet up with Nate. We watch Nate leave to take his phone call.

My stomach twists in knots when I walk away—and stop. I look to my left.

Troy stops the footage there and rotates the camera angle. It doesn't show anything down the hall.

He switches to a different camera in a different part of the concourse. He has to expand the feed—and we all look straight down the hall into the storeroom.

I relive that moment of horror as Carlos crams his hips between Alexis's legs, pulls her ass back and forth across the table to match his thrusts, and snarls and growls in her face in raw, brutal lust.

Nate turns away. I feel for him. I rest my hand on his arm just to let him know he isn't alone.

"Can we get a copy of this?" I ask.

"Sure." Troy goes through a few different combinations of maneuvers on his computer. "Give me your email addresses and I'll send it to both of you."

Nate turns around. He barely makes a sound when he gives Troy the address.

"We really appreciate it," I tell Troy. "You're a lifesaver."

"Let me know if you need anything else."

I steer Nate out of the security office and back out onto the deck. The sunshine clears my head. Now I have the proof I need to confront Carlos the right way. I won't let him weasel out this time.

"Are you gonna be okay?" I ask Nate once we get outside.

He won't look at me. He stares over the ship's rail at nothing. "Yeah. I'll be fine. I already knew she did it. I felt it in my gut. I shouldn't have let her get into my head."

"What are you going to do?"

"I don't know," he mumbles. "I need to take some time to figure that out."

"I'm so sorry you have to go through this. I don't say that because I blame myself. I just wish it didn't have to be this way."

He straightens up and faces me. "I'm really grateful to you—for everything. Thank you—for being here. I couldn't do this without you. If there's anything I can do....."

I look down at the deck, but the boards blur when tears spring to my eyes. "No one can do anything for me."

"Hey!" he murmurs. "You did the right thing. You have nothing to be ashamed of. He's an asshole for doing this to you."

"You don't understand!" I look around everywhere. I can't hold back tears. "We were supposed to get pregnant on this trip! I just want to start a family.....and now that's gone! I have to split up with him.....which means I have to start over with someone else.....It isn't fair!"

I start really crying. Nate pulls me in and hugs me. "You're right. It isn't fair," he murmurs into my hair. "You did everything right. You're going to make some guy very happy someday. You're smart, beautiful, resourceful, and kind. You're everything a guy could ask for. He's a chump for treating you like this. You're better off without him."

He pushes me back. I wipe my cheeks, but that doesn't stop me from crying. "My life is in the toilet," I grumble.

"That makes two of us. You have my number, right? You call me if anything happens or you need help with anything."

I nod, but I'm too devastated to deal with Nate right now.

His kindness feels like such an insult. I should have been able to count on that kind of support from my husband.

Now I'm going home to a divorce. This cruise is turning into my worst nightmare.

Chapter 7: Nate

A strange sense of calm comes over me when I enter the suite I share with Alexis—the suite I used to share with Alexis.

I look around. I have no desire even to be on the same continent with Alexis anymore, much less stay in the same room with her.

I do need to confront her, though. I need to do that for myself.

I go into the bedroom, pack my suitcase, and move it to the other bedroom—the one I stayed in last night. I leave my suitcase on the bed and sit down on the couch.

I pull out my phone, contact the ship's purser, and arrange to rent a different suite for the duration of the cruise. Alexis has already destroyed my life with her antics. I don't plan to let her destroy my vacation, too.

I'm still sitting there tapping on my phone when she comes in. She smiles at me in her usual predatory way. I sure was blinded by her body if I didn't see what a shark she is.

"I thought you would keep avoiding me for the rest of the week," she remarks.

"I'm not trying to avoid you," I tell her. "Not at all."

She comes over to me and sits down sideways on my lap. She wraps her arms around my neck. "So are you ready to give me that apology yet?"

"Yes, I am. Here it is." I raise my phone and start playing the camera footage of her and Carlos.

She takes one look at it and shoots off my lap. "You bastard!" she blares. "You have no right to sit in judgment of me."

"It sure looks like I do. You lied through your teeth last night. God only knows how many times you've been banging random guys behind mind back while I've been out of town. How many was it—a hundred? Two hundred? Five hundred?"

"It's your fault!" she snaps. "You left me completely alone!"

My blood turns to ice water in my veins. "My fault?! You are not blaming me for this!"

"I was alone!" she roars. "You left town for weeks at a time! What did you think I was going to do?"

"Oh, I don't know! How about honor your marriage vows? How about keep your panties on for a little while until I came back? Do you think I was out there banging everything that walks because you weren't there?!"

"You might have been! What difference does it make? What's good for the goose is good for the gander."

I stare at her as the horrific truth sinks in. "You've been doing this the whole time, haven't you? You've been cheating on me ever since we got married."

"You should have been there!" she blares. "You weren't there to give it to me. I have needs, you know! I had to get it from somewhere and you weren't there!"

"I wasn't there because I was out there earning the money to pay for that house you said you needed so badly! You would rather keep that house than stay married to me! I only did that job at all to give you what you wanted!" Another penny drops in my mind. "This is why you didn't want me to get a local job, isn't it? You wanted to keep playing the field while I paid all your expenses."

"You're an asshole!" she fires back. "You never gave me what I needed."

"I'm an asshole for staying loyal to you for as long as I did." I stand up. "Don't worry. I won't be that kind of asshole anymore."

I walk into the other room, take my suitcase off the bed, set it on its wheels, and steer it into the living room.

She frowns at me. "What are you doing?"

"I'm leaving. I'm moving to another suite for the rest of the cruise. We'll both start handling our affairs. I'll cut off your bank account--and make sure you move out of my house when you get back to town. I'll contact my lawyer about starting the divorce process—and don't worry. I'll be including this footage so you don't get any alimony or compensation from the divorce."

I take two steps toward the door before she lunges into my path. "Stop, Nate! You can't leave."

"I can and I will.".

"You can't do this! You can't just dump me like this."

"Why not? You said I was an asshole for trying to be a good husband to you. So clearly the right thing to do is to not do that anymore."

I try to step around her, but she swerves in front of me again. "We can work this out, Nate. This is all a big misunderstanding...."

"Which part of you spreading your legs for another man did I misunderstand? The footage seems pretty straightforward to me."

"I just needed you when you were gone all the time. Things would be different if you got a local job...."

"But you don't want me to get a local job. You said you didn't want to give up the house. Now you're giving up the house and me and your bank account and everything. I hope you're happy."

I walk around her again. She grabs my arm to hold me back. "Nate—wait!"

I don't stop. I shake her off as gently as I can and push my suitcase to the door.

"Nate!" she yells again.

I ignore her, steer my suitcase out in the hall, and let the door swing shut just as she screams again, "NATE!!"

I walk away. I don't have to deal with this crap any longer. I head for my new suite, unlock the door, and put my suitcase on the bed in the bedroom.

I choose the righthand bedroom. It's the other bedroom—not the one where Alexis stayed in the other suite. I never want to go over there again, not even when it's in another suite.

I park my suitcase, sink down on the mattress, and bury my face in my hands, now that I'm completely alone.

The whole terrible episode comes crashing down on my head. It's over. I have to divorce her. I have to go through the whole ugly legal process of stopping her bank account and probably changing the locks on my house.

At least the house is in my name. She can't claim any of my assets. I can throw her out on her ass where she belongs, but that doesn't make this any easier.

I want to crumble into a hole and never come out. I want to let my whole life fall apart, but I can't. I have to hold it together.

I get on my phone and contact a car dealership in Seattle. They agree to go out to my house, transport her car to their lot, and sell it for me. The car is in my name, too, so she can't stop me.

Then I cancel my usual transfers of spending money to her account. She should start feeling the pinch even before she gets off this cruise. Good. The lying, manipulative witch.

I feel like a fool for letting her take me in. I should have seen her for what she was. That was my fault. I let her blind me with sex and her beauty.

Now I have nothing left—nothing but my job and my empty life without her.

Chapter 8: Holly

I lean over the balcony and look down at the rear deck below my suite. People walk back and forth across the deck. Couples lounge against the rail with their arms around each other.

Do any of those people have a clue how disastrously wrong their relationships could go—literally overnight? Do any of those people suspect their partners of cheating?

I pull out my phone and stare at it. I can think of a lot of things to do on this phone, but I don't seem to be able to do any of them.

Carlos and I already have separate bank accounts. All my pay goes into my bank account. I don't have to do anything to separate that.

I also own my car, so that's taken care of, too.

We jointly own our house. We won't be able to divide that—not without selling it. All our other assets are held separately. I shouldn't be able to claim anything from him and he shouldn't be able to claim anything from me.

Something must have told me not to mingle our assets. What would have happened if we really did have children and I had to stop working? How would that have worked with Carlos paying one hundred percent of our mortgage payments?

That is never going to happen now. I need to work out a place for myself to live once I get home from the cruise. I'll never go back to that house again.

I can't bring myself to do that now. I stick my phone in my pocket.

I want to purge the video of Carlos and Alexis. I don't want it on my phone anymore, but I have to keep it there until I show it to him. I can't let him lie to me anymore.

I don't even know how I'm going to look him in the face long enough to confront him. I never want to see the scumbag again.

I should probably move out of this suite, but I can't even summon the resolve to do that. I can't bring myself to think right now—about anything.

He stays out for a long time. Is he out there knocking them down one after the other as fast as he can?

Sweet Jesus, what the hell did I get myself into? How did someone I loved and trusted so much turn out to be such a scum-sucking dirtbag?

It's a good thing Nate and I didn't make arrangements for him and Alexis to have dinner with me and Carlos. Carlos comes in so late that we wouldn't have made it in time.

I'm still on the balcony looking out at the ocean when I hear the door open and close behind me. I don't turn around. How can I lower myself even to look at this cocksucker?

He comes up behind me and actually has the nerve to put his arm around me. "Where would you like to go for dinner tonight?"

"I don't know where I'll go or what I'll do for dinner tonight, but I know one thing for certain. You're going to be going straight to Hell itself."

He jolts back. "What's the matter now?"

I turn around to face him. I don't even try to pull out of his arms. "You screwed around with Alexis. You don't have to lie about it because I already know."

He jerks away and storms back into the suite. "Not that again! I told you it was someone else.'

"I saw you," I call after him. "She spread her legs on the table in the supply room behind the Chinese restaurant. Just admit it. Don't make it worse by lying about it again."

"You're insane!" he yells over his shoulder. "You're hallucinating."

"Was I hallucinating when I got Troy Nixon to pull up security camera footage from the concourse? Was I hallucinating when he sent the footage to my phone and also to Nate's phone so he could confront Alexis about it? Was I hallucinating then?"

Carlos spins around and narrows his eyes at me. "You're making that up."

I pull out my phone and scroll to the footage. I don't play it. I just pull up a still of the shot from the concourse. That's enough.

I show it to him.

He explodes in a flurry of activity. "It wasn't what you think!" he yells over his shoulder on his way into the bedroom.

I follow him in there. "How can it not be what I think? Did you stick your prick inside her or not? We came on this cruise so we could get pregnant and start a family—not so you could play the field with a bunch of women you don't even know!"

"That has nothing to do with it!" he snaps.

"How can it not have anything to do with it? You cheated on me!"

He spins around and waves in my face. "You're the one who couldn't get pregnant! You can't blame me for not trying!"

"We don't know if I'm the one who can't get pregnant! We've both had multiple checkups. Nothing is wrong with either of us! It's as likely to be something wrong with you as something wrong with me."

"Well, I never wanted to have children anyway!" he blurts out. "I never asked for any of this!"

I gape at him and my blood runs cold. "You don't? Why didn't you say so?"

"What was I supposed to say—that I don't want kids at all? You would have hit the roof."

"I would have hit the roof a lot less than I am right now when I find out you've been lying to me for years! I asked you when we were dating if you wanted kids, Carlos—when we were dating!! You said yes! You've been harping on all this time about how you wanted kids! Was our whole marriage a lie?!"

Why do I even ask that? Of course our whole marriage was a lie. What else would it be?

He spins away. "I'm not going to talk to you about this. You don't know what you're talking about."

I stare in horror as he pulls his suitcase out of the closet. "What are you doing?"

"I'm moving out of the suite. I'm moving in with Alexis."

I open my mouth, but no sound comes out. This isn't happening.

I can only stand and stare as he pitches all his stuff in his suitcase. I should talk to him about the house and the divorce we're going to have and all of that.

I can't say a word. I can't move. I can't feel a thing.

He zips his suitcase shut and actually has the audacity to kiss me on the cheek before he wheels his suitcase out of the room. The door slams shut. I'm alone. It's over.

I stumble out into the living room and sink onto the couch. I can't think of anything except that I'll sleep on the couch for the rest of the cruise.

I don't know if that will help me kickstart my brain into gear. I don't know if my brain will ever restart again.

He never wanted children. He lied to me about everything. He lied to me from day one.

He must have sensed that I wouldn't stay with him if he said he didn't want kids. He concocted this whole scheme to rope me into a lie.

All these years I've been married to him—it was all a giant waste of time. I could have gotten together with someone else—someone who really wanted to have kids.

Now what am I going to do? I'm single. Am I supposed to go on a bunch of dating sites to try to find someone else? I can't think of a worse nightmare.

I thought I found the man of my dreams. Now I find out he's a monster.

Chapter 9: Nate

I come out of the elevator and head for the pool, but I stop when I spot Holly standing on the rear deck.

Not many people go out there. It's a good place to go if you want to be alone.

She stands with her back to the world and stares over the side at the ship's wake churning behind the boat. She looks so lonely.

I go out there and stop next to her. "Hey. How are you doing?" I ask.

She doesn't look up. "I really don't know," she mumbles. "I don't know how I'm doing. I don't think I can feel anything."

"Have you seen Carlos and Alexis since the big upheaval?"

"This is the first time I've left my suite since it happened."

I spin around to stare at her. "That was three days ago! What have you been doing in there by yourself?"

She shrugs. "Feeling sorry for myself, I guess. I've been eating room service and staring into space. That's about it."

I look away. Damn. This is bad. Her breakup with Carlos must have hit her hard.

"He said he never wanted kids," she murmurs. "He lied to me since we first started dating. Our whole marriage was a lie. I guess I've just been trying to process the fact that I gave the best years of my life to such a piece of shit. All of that time….wasted. Now I have to start over from scratch with someone else. It could take me years to deal with this. I might not be fertile at all by the time I'm ready to get with someone else."

"You will be," I tell her, though I don't know why I believe this. "You'll find someone. You'll be happy. I'm certain of it."

"I don't even know how to start over. Isn't that pathetic?" She shrugs that away. "What about you? Are you okay? You moved out of your suite, didn't you? Carlos and Alexis are living together in your old place."

"Yes, I moved out. She blamed me, said she was lonely while I was out of town, and said it would have been okay with her if I cheated on her while I was gone." I shake my head. "I just don't know what's going on in their heads. I took a vow. I plan to stick to it."

"I think I might leave the ship," she tells me.

"What?!" I exclaim. "Don't do that! Don't cut your trip short."

"What's the point in staying—so I can see them together? I want to put all of this behind me and that means moving out of my house, getting my own place, and getting the divorce moving. Staying here just feels like an even bigger waste of time."

"Don't leave," I insist. "I need someone to commiserate with. Look at all these happy couples all over the place. I need someone who is as miserable and bitter as I am."

She actually laughs. "You make a good case."

"Anyway, it will give you some time to think about everything before you have to go back and deal with all that business. Are you gonna be okay financially?"

She nods. "Everything is already separate except for the house. That should be pretty straightforward. What about you?"

"Yep. I own the house, her car, and I was transferring money to her bank account every month for her to spend. I can stop all of that and use the infidelity to make sure she doesn't get any more."

"That's good. I'm glad you're protected."

"I won't make that mistake again. It's going to be a long time before I'm ready to get into another relationship. I might stay single for life. Things are so much simpler this way."

"I wish I could do that, but I can't. I want children and I was ready to do that before this happened."

"I'm sure you'll find someone," I tell her. "Plenty of guys want to have kids—like they *really* want them and aren't just saying that to tie you down."

She looks away, but not before I see her cheek spasm. "He said our infertility problems were my fault. What if he's right? What if there really is something wrong with me and I can't have children at all?"

"Don't listen to that. He was just messing with your head again."

"I don't know," she breathes. "We tried for months and failed every time. How would I really know?"

"And you went through all the medical testing and everything?"

She nods. "Nothing turned up."

I find myself looking away again. This conversation strikes a chord.

"I shouldn't be pushing all my negativity on you," she goes on. "Let's talk about something else. You won't have to worry about getting a local job now."

"Maybe I should." The words don't stop once they start. "I wanted to start a family, too. That's why I wanted to get a local job—so we could start. Now I don't even know if I want that—but then I would be alone for the rest of my life. I would be the uncle who stays single all his life. I can't decide which is better." I pass my hand across my eyes. "I really needed to snap out of it and stop being so jaded and cynical.

I should just knuckle down and find a woman who wants to have a family, but I don't know how I would do that when I travel so much for work."

"Maybe you should take the local job first and then start screening for applicants."

Now I'm the one who laughs. "Don't make me laugh. I'm trying to be depressed over here."

She beams at me, but it isn't her old beaming smile.

I find myself smiling back at her. "I like talking to you. Have dinner with me tonight. I need someone who understands my cynicism."

She blushes. "Okay. Why not?"

"What do you have planned for the rest of the day?"

"More room service and staring at the wall. I only came down here to get some sunshine. Then I'm going back to my crypt."

I snort. "That sounds bad. Maybe I shouldn't be going out with someone undead."

"You definitely shouldn't—but at least I'm not completely dead. That would be terrible."

"Seriously," I ask her. "What are you going to do about the rest of the cruise?"

"If I go home now, I suppose I'll just be staring at the wall there, too. So there isn't really a point in me going home just yet. Whatever I would do now I'll wind up doing then anyway. It doesn't really matter whether I stay or go. I have no reason to do either."

"Then will you stay because I asked you to? Is that enough of a reason?"

She blushes at me. "I like talking to you, too. It's nice to talk to someone who understands."

"I'm really glad you're here," I tell her. "You've been solid in my corner every step of the way. I'm really grateful for everything you're doing."

"Aw," she mutters. "I'm not really doing anything except trying to get through the day."

I wave to one side. "Sit down. Talk to me for a while."

"Isn't that what I'm doing?"

I lead the way to one of the benches on the side of the deck. I sit down and she sits next to me.

"Talk to me," I tell her. "Tell me about something....your family... ..anything."

"How's *your* family?" she asks. "How's your mom?"

"She's okay. She's recovering at home. The procedure seems to be working. She has more energy and she can walk around the house without getting exhausted."

"That's great. I'm glad she came through it."

"My brothers have been helping my dad out. I feel bad for not being there, but they all insist that I finish my vacation. They think Alexis and I are having a wonderful, romantic interlude together. I hate to think what they'll say when they find out what really happened."

She snorts. "That sounds like my family—minus the heart condition."

"Does your family live in Spokane?"

"They actually live in Seattle. I'm from there."

I spin around. "No way!"

"Are you originally from Seattle?" she asks.

"Yes. I went to Jefferson High School."

"No dice. I went to Charleston High School and then I went to Cornell."

My jaw drops. "You went to Cornell."

She grins at me and nods. "Bow down, mere peasants."

I shake my head. "Now I feel really inferior."

She won't stop beaming at me. "You don't have to. There's nothing superior about me now. I'm a troll who never leaves my house—except when I go grocery shopping. I'm just a desk jockey like all the others. I'm sure my job is some people's idea of Hell."

"I'm sure my job is, too."

I find myself resisting the urge to put my arm around her. Spending time with her feels so good. It's effortless and easy—but it also leaves me feeling energized and hopeful in ways I haven't felt since this whole Alexis thing blew up.

I smile back at her. Smiling at her comes naturally—like it was meant to be. "Do you feel better now?" I ask.

"Yeah," she breathes. "Thanks. I'm really glad you're here. I would definitely leave if I didn't have you to talk to."

"I'll stop by your place around seven and pick you up for dinner."

She laughs. "You'll pick me up in your car and drive me down the hall to the elevator."

"I could throw you over my shoulder and carry you down to the concourse that way."

She blushes and her eyelashes dip. She really is beautiful. "Let's just walk, okay?"

"I don't know....." I go on. "Throwing you over my shoulder sounds pretty good about now. That would certainly make Carlos and Alexis talk, wouldn't it?"

She laughs again. "I think I better get out of this conversation before it turns into something neither of us is prepared for. I'll see you tonight, okay?"

"Okay. Be there or be square."

She laughs again, says a quick, "Bye," and leaves.

I turn around on the bench and stare out over the ocean. I sure do like spending time with her. I don't feel like I'm on trial or that I'm escorting a movie star around town.

She's just a normal person, but everything about her is so pure and good and easy. I just want to keep hanging out with her.

Her presence makes this all okay because she understands. I don't have to pretend that I'm on a romantic cruise with my wife because I'm with Holly instead.

She makes me not care so much about Alexis. Alexis is already in my past because I have something so much better to do.

Chapter 10: Holly

N ate knocks on my door at seven o'clock on the nose. I open it and find him standing there in the classy suit he wore that first night when Carlos and I had dinner with Nate and Alexis.

His eyes skim down to my dress. I'm wearing a close-fitting, jewel-tone, deep green velvet dress with a sweetheart neckline, wide, off-the-shoulder sleeves, and a mermaid hem.

This dress shows off my curves better than any other dress I've ever owned. Nate has definitely never seen me like this before.

His eyes drop out of their sockets. He stares at me in wordless shock.

I laugh and blush at his reaction when I step out of the suite and pull the door shut behind me. "I'm going to take that as a compliment. Are you ready to go? I'll assume you are since you're here. Blink twice if you can hear me."

He shakes himself back to his senses and offers me his arm on our way down the hall toward the elevator. "Sorry. Something just hit me over the head with a croquet mallet."

"My sister hit my brother over the head with a croquet mallet when they were younger."

"No kidding? Why did she do that?"

"I don't know. It's been a joke in our family ever since. Someone is always bringing it up. It has become an inside joke in our family like, 'If you lay a finger on my slice of cheesecake, I'm going to hit you over the head with a croquet mallet,' or 'Oh, you forgot to buy butter at the grocery store? Did someone hit you over the head with a croquet mallet?'"

He laughs. "Nice."

"Someone brought it up again at our most recent holiday gathering and I asked my sister why she did it. She said, 'I don't remember. He probably won.'"

His eyes twinkle at me. "Just don't hit me over the head with a croquet mallet if I piss you off."

"You're in luck. I didn't bring one in my luggage for this cruise."

"Too bad. You could have used it on Carlos."

Now it's my turn to laugh. "Maybe I should have been using it on him all these years to keep him in line."

We have to stop talking when other people get into the elevator with us, but Nate won't stop smiling at me.

Part of me feels like I'm doing something wrong by going out to dinner with a man other than my husband. I have to keep reminding myself that I'm not married to Carlos anymore except on paper.

Besides, I haven't done anything with Nate. We just talked and that's all we're doing now. We're supporting each other through a disastrous situation.

I sure do like him. He's so easy to get along with. I never have to worry about him doing anything underhanded or hiding anything or trying to pull anything on me.

He's so solid and reliable. Alexis probably found that boring in him, but I find it incredibly attractive.

He's an incredibly handsome man anyway, but that aspect of his personality really shines through. He stayed loyal to Alexis all those years. He supported her and gave her everything she wanted.

She's an idiot for throwing away such a good man. She probably doesn't even realize how good and stable and supportive he is.

We enter the concourse and ride the escalator to the third floor. He leads the way into one of the nicer restaurants. I haven't been here before.

Everyone in here is dressed up as nicely as we are. We fit right in, but we look like a couple. The maître d' treats us like one.

I keep expecting Nate to put his arm around me like we're on a date. I guess we are on a date considering the way we're both dressed.

He pulls out my chair for me to help me sit down. He orders a bottle of wine and then gazes at me across the table. "This is so nice," he tells me. "You make this whole thing so much more tolerable."

"Thanks. I could say the same thing about you."

"So what will you do when you get home—besides moving out of your house and getting your own place?"

I make a face. "I really don't want to go back onto the dating market, but I suppose I have to. I'll have to be extremely specific with everyone that I'm only looking for something serious and that I want to start a family. That should eliminate ninety-eight percent of the dating pool."

He snorts. "You can say that again. Just don't say the M word to anyone or they might start throwing holy water and garlic at you."

I laugh. "At least they won't hit me over the head with a croquet mallet, right?"

He laughs, too. "We wouldn't want that."

The waiter brings the wine and Nate pours for both of us. We order and the waiter leaves us alone again.

I catch Nate giving me a significant look over his wine glass. Is he thinking of us as a possible couple?

"What about you?" I ask. "What will you do when you get home? You don't have to move out of your house or anything. It doesn't sound like you need to change anything."

That makes him look down at the wine swirling in his glass. "No, you're right. I don't have to do anything. I'll just go straight back to work. The only difference is that I won't have Alexis to come home to when I finish each trip. That will suck, but at least I won't have to worry about her getting bored or running around on me behind my back."

"Do you think you'll date?"

"I don't know. I should probably wait and figure out if I want that and what I really do want."

"Good idea. It's never a good idea to go on the market if you don't know what you want."

He looks up at me and says something, but I don't hear it. My blood turns to ice when I look past him toward the restaurant entrance.

He sees my reaction right away. "What's wrong?" he asks.

He finds out when he follows my gaze to Carlos and Alexis strolling into the same restaurant with their arms around each other.

Carlos wears his mid-level suit. Alexis wears one of her world-stopping Marilyn Monroe dresses.

Their presence casts a chill over me and Nate. He turns his back on them and glares down at his wine glass. His features turn to granite again. "Ignore them," he snarls. "Don't pay any attention to them."

I try to look at him or my wine glass, too, but my gaze keeps getting drawn to Carlos and Alexis.

She laughs loudly when they sit down at their table. Sitting down shows off every inch of her stunning body. Other men in the restaurant turn around to look at her. They have a hard time tearing their eyes away from her, too.

Nate breaks in on my thoughts. He's lucky he's sitting with his back to them. He just has to sit there and he won't see them.

"Look at me," he murmurs. "Talk to me. Don't think about them."

"It's kinda hard not to. I'm looking straight at them."

"Just remember they're both cheaters. They're incapable of doing anything other than sleeping around. They'll wind up cheating on each other."

I smile at him. He always makes me feel better. "Which one of them do you think will cave first?"

"I bet you a hundred dollars Carlos caves first."

"Oh, no fair!" I howl. "I was going to bet on Carlos, too."

Nate finally smiles again. "Great minds think alike, huh? What do you think will happen after that? How much do you want to bet they come crawling back to us begging for another chance?"

"Let's make a pact never to take them back. We'll have to keep each other strong."

His eyes twinkle and he sticks out his pinky finger. "Pinky promise."

I hook my little finger around his and squeeze. "Pinky promise."

We both sink back into our chairs smiling at each other—until my eyes swivel toward Carlos's and Alexis's table.

They're sitting right next to each other in a booth with their arms around each other. They start kissing and making out right there at the table.

He slides his hand up her ribs and barely stops himself from squeezing her breast. He better not start groping her in public.

Nate's expression changes when he sees what I'm looking at. "This sucks," he mutters. "Maybe we should go to another restaurant."

"We can't," I mutter. "We already ordered."

Like magic, the waiter comes with our order right then. He distracts us for a minute and then we start eating.

Carlos and Alexis talk and laugh loudly enough for Nate and me to hear them over all the other noise in the restaurant. The sound dampens any enjoyment I could have gotten from spending time with Nate.

We don't talk anymore during the meal. I really wish we could leave, but I don't want to give Carlos and Alexis the satisfaction of robbing Nate and me of our evening together.

Carlos and Alexis are already robbing Nate and me of our evening together. They completely destroy the atmosphere.

We finish our meal in silence and leave the restaurant in silence. I'm walking down the concourse with my head in the clouds when Nate takes my hand. He pulls it through his elbow and presses it into his arm.

"I'm really glad you're here." His eyes overflow with warmth when they look down at me. "I'm glad I have you to spend time with and talk to. I would hate to go through this alone."

"I feel the same way about you. I'm sorry tonight fell so flat."

"We should probably get used to seeing them around the ship. We won't get away from them as long as we're stuck at sea with them."

"I know," I murmur. "That's why I stayed locked in my suite so much, but I can't really keep doing that."

"Let's hang out together tomorrow. We can keep each other company even if we can't avoid seeing them."

"I'd like that." We stop in front of my suite and face each other. "Thank you for taking me out tonight. I really enjoyed the first part of it when we were by ourselves."

"Let's work on it until we can enjoy ourselves all the time, even when those two scumbags are in the same room with us."

I find myself smiling. "I would really like that. Thank you for being there for me."

"Likewise." He holds out his arms. "Can I give you a hug?"

I hug him. He's so big and strong and solid. Hugging him feels good.

He pulls back and smiles at me. "I'd like to consider you a friend. I trust you in ways I haven't trusted hardly anyone in my life outside my own family."

"I consider you a friend, too. I really appreciate your support. I need it." I pull away. "Good night."

He takes a step back and says, "Good night," before we part for the evening.

Chapter 11: Nate

I walk into my suite and start taking off my suit. Going out to dinner with Holly is so good for the soul.

She's going to be pivotal in me getting over Alexis. I would probably try to hurt someone if I saw Carlos and Alexis in public when I didn't have Holly there to balance me out.

Supporting her calms me down. It normalizes all of this and softens the blow.

I can't wait to see her again tomorrow. Just being friends with her and being there for each other is the best thing that has come out of all of this.

I'm just changing into my pajamas when my phone rings. It's a video call from my brother, Liam.

I sit down on my bed to answer it. His face appears on the screen. He's bigger than I am even though he's two years younger.

His hair and eyes are lighter, but other than that, we resemble each other. People thought we were twins growing up.

"Hey, man," I tell him. "How are the old people?"

"Mom is still improving and getting stronger. She actually cleaned the damn fridge today and she says she's going to clean out the kitchen cabinets tomorrow, so that tells you how she feels about staying home from work."

I laugh. "Good for her. I'm glad she's bouncing back."

"Dad isn't doing so good. He came down with the flu yesterday. I think the stress of Mom having the procedure weakened him, so he's in bed drunk out of his mind on Nyquil."

I laugh again. "Even better. Sedate him until it passes."

"How's the cruise? I need to take Sandy on one of those next year."

I nod. "Good idea."

"So what is it like? Are you and Alexis doing all the activities or staying locked in your room around the clock?"

I wince. I can't tell him the truth.

Then I throw all my inhibitions out the window. My family is going to find out the truth eventually. Why lie about it now?

He sees my reaction. His tone changes instantly. "What's the matter?" he growls.

"That first night—right after we left the pier—we met up with another couple in a restaurant. We had dinner with them and then I was walking around alone on the concourse the next day while Alexis got a massage. I bumped into the woman of this other couple. Her name is Holly and her husband is Carlos. We talked and I invited them out for dinner a second time."

"Nothing wrong with that. It sounds like you're having a good time."

"You don't understand. Our conversation got interrupted when you called me about Mom. I went off to answer it, and after I hung up, I bumped into Holly again. She got super agitated and upset and said she just spotted Carlos and Alexis doing it in some side hallway of the ship."

His jaw drops. "Doing it. As in—screwing each other?"

I nod. "I didn't know what to think. She was going out of her mind—and so was I. We agreed to confront the two of them—and we did."

"What did they say?"

"They both denied it up and down. Alexis even said I owed her an apology for accusing her when Holly obviously made a mistake about what she saw. Holly and I both started to doubt ourselves. We met back up and then we checked with the ship's Chief of Security. He tracked down security camera footage of them doing it. It was all real. It turns out they've both been cheating the whole time—like the whole time we've been married."

His hand flies to his head. "Oh, my God! I am so sorry! Do you want to come home? I'm sure they have procedures for people who need to leave the ship early?"

"No, I can't leave. I need to get my head clear about what I'm doing with my life. I moved to another suit, but we keep seeing Carlos and Alexis together all over the boat. They're all over each other and won't keep their hands off each other. They even moved into the same suite together."

"Man! That is terrible."

"I need to ask you a favor. I don't want to get you in the middle of this, but you're there and I'm here."

"Name it, brother," he tells me. "Anything you need, I'm your boy."

"I need you to go to my house and see if you can find any evidence of her infidelity. I have the footage from the boat, but I need proof that she was doing it the rest of the time—like every time I went out of town. I don't know where you would find this, but I really need your help right now."

"You got it, man," he tells me. "I'll find it. Leave it to me."

"Thanks, bro. I really appreciate it."

We wish each other good night and I stretch out in bed. I turn off the light and stare at the stars outside my balcony.

Now my family knows. He'll tell everyone else. My parents, my brothers, and their families will all find out in the next couple of days. No one can keep a secret in my family.

At least I won't have to explain anything to them. They'll all understand when I divorce Alexis and stop bringing her around my family.

It sure does suck, though. It sucks that she played me for a chump when I thought I was doing the right thing for her.

It sucks that I have to go through an ugly divorce with her. It sucks that I'll be working as a traveling salesman with no home or family to go back to.

Maybe I should sell my house and not buy another one. Maybe I should just go on the road and live without roots for a while before I settle down with someone else.

I'm not getting any younger, though. I really wanted to start a family with Alexis. I was looking forward to that. Now I'm not so sure if I even want it.

I should have known when she kept putting it off and coming up with excuses not to go through with it. That should have been my first clue.

It's over now. I turn over and fall asleep.

I wake up the next morning to my phone ringing. I sit up in bed to check the screen. It's Liam.

I'm still rubbing the sleep out of my eyes when I answer the video call. "What's going on?" I ask. "It's six o'clock in the morning, man."

"It's six o'clock in the evening here, pal, remember? You're on the other side of the world."

"What's up? Are Mom and Dad okay?"

"Forget all that. I found the evidence you asked for—the evidence that Alexis was sleeping around every time you went out of town."

My brain clears in a split second. "What did you find?"

"It took me about ten minutes to find everything you asked for. All I had to do was knock on the door of the house across the street. The dude who owns the house has security cameras all over the house and yard. He has a driveway cam that points toward your house. The footage recorded men pulling up to the house and even caught plenty of imagery through the living room and bedroom windows. It's all there, brother. He even let me copy the footage. I have it all on a memory stick waiting for you."

I sink back on the bed. "I don't know if I can be happy about that."

"You shouldn't be, but at least now you know. I'm telling you, bro. There were at least three hundred guys. We had to fast-forward through the footage. We stopped counting after two hundred and twenty and there was still a mind-blowing amount of footage left. You won't have any problem proving her infidelity if this goes to court or anything like that."

I run my fingers through my hair. "Um....thanks.....I guess....."

"You're welcome. I'm going to put the memory stick in my safe deposit box. That's where it will be and that's where it will stay until you come home and decide to do something about this."

"Thanks, man. I really appreciate it."

"Anything. Don't hesitate to come on home if you need to. I'll call you later and check on you."

He hangs up again. I fall back into the bed, roll onto my side, and stare out through the balcony doors.

This is nothing I didn't already know about. It's just confirmation of what Alexis already told me she was doing.

This changes things. I don't know how, but it does.

Chapter 12: Holly

I meet up with Nate in the piazza. "So what do you want to do today?" he asks. "This place has everything."

"We could play golf or racquetball or something like that. Carlos does rock climbing, so I would prefer not to do that. Or we could do something sedentary like watch a movie or catch a show."

"Do you like racquetball?" he asks.

"Sure, I like it."

"Are you any good at it?"

I smirk at him. "What's the matter? Are you worried I'm going to beat you?"

"Just don't hit me over the head with your racquet if I win."

I laugh. "It's a deal. Let's go."

We head upstairs to the ship's gym. A bunch of people are in there working out. We pass the rowing machines and elliptical trainers before we enter the racquetball courts.

Nate and I spend the whole game joking around, talking trash to each other, and getting all sweaty. We both have to go to our suites to change before we meet back up for lunch.

"Let's see a show after this," he tells me. "Musical, theatrical, cinema, or music? It's your choice."

"Let's go with cinema."

"Good choice." We go to the concourse and get burgers for lunch.

We take them out onto the deck and sit on a bench to eat. That's when we see Carlos and Alexis near the pool.

They're joined at the lips again with their tongues down each other's throats and their hands all over each other.

They see us watching them and throw themselves at each other even harder. They keep shooting me and Nate vindictive sneers while Carlos and Alexis rub themselves all over each other.

"I'm surprised she doesn't stick her hand down his shorts and give him a hand-job right here in public," I snarl.

"She probably does it in out of the way corners and public bathrooms," he adds. "That's the kind of trashy thing she would do."

I force myself to look down at my fries. "She better hope he's the one who was infertile."

"She's on birth control. She had to be when she was entertaining all those guys at my house while I was out of town."

"Are you sure she actually did it?"

"Oh, yeah. I asked my brother to look into it. He got security camera footage from the house across the street. She had a regular parade of guys coming through my house. I wouldn't be surprised to find out they were paying her for it."

"Wow. That is absolutely awful."

"The only good thing is that my brother got the recordings. He's saving them for me to use in the divorce, so I don't have to worry about that."

I look out at the ocean while I sip my milkshake. "Maybe I should do some digging into Carlos's activities."

"You should. Let me know if you want any help with that."

I don't answer. I can't unthink these thoughts, now that they're actually passing through my mind.

Nate and I finish eating. Then we go see a movie. It's the stupidest, cheapest, most idiotic B-movie imaginable, but it's the perfect solution to take our minds off our troubles.

We agree to meet back up for dinner that night. We even see Carlos and Alexis staggering to the elevator.

"They're probably on their way back to their suite right now," I mutter.

"They can have each other. I'll pick you up at seven again, okay?"

I smile at him and don't make any more snide remarks about him picking me up. "Okay. See you then."

We both go upstairs and part toward our own suites.

All my doubts and suspicions erupt back to life the minute I shut the door. What was Carlos doing behind my back? Did he have a parade of women going through our house?

He couldn't have because I work from home. I was there every day. He must have done it somewhere else.

I need proof. Where can I get it if I can't get security camera footage from the house across the street?

He works as a hospital administrator. He's at work all day every day. He must have been doing it there.

Hospitals are notorious breeding grounds for cheating and interpersonal drama. He could have been banging all the staff—or maybe even the patients and their loved ones.

I cringe at the thought, but I have to find out. I get on the internet and start scouring our records for the slightest clue.

My first thought is to check our bank account records. Carlos and I have separate bank accounts and I don't have access to his account.

I do have access to some of his other internet accounts—less sensitive accounts. I also know he's one of those guys who uses the same password for everything.

I get onto his bank account website and try to log into his account. The password works and takes me to a second verification page.

The page asks me to enter his father's middle name. Of course I already know that. It's Ricardo.

The second verification question asks me the name of the city Carlos was born in. I know that, too. This is too easy.

I enter the name and it opens his bank account records. I start scrolling through hundreds of transactions.

All the recent activity on his account is on board the ship. I skip to before that.

I don't see anything except a whole bunch of business dinners and other work-related stuff. He has to do all of that for his job. Nothing leaps out at me.

I freeze when I see a charge of eight hundred dollars from Maldonado's Fine Jewelers. The date is one month before we went on the cruise.

He never bought me any jewelry from there. He didn't buy me any jewelry from anywhere. I would remember that.

Then I find a charge for an expensive lingerie boutique in Seattle. He didn't buy me any lingerie, either.

I screenshot one transaction after another. I could probably get into trouble for hacking his bank account records, but we are still technically married.

I work my way through page after page of transactions and save all the screenshots to my cloud storage. I don't know if these will come in handy later, but at least I have proof now.

I'm just about to shut it down and go take a hot shower to wash off the taint of seeing everything he's been doing all these years. God only knows how far back this goes.

I should find out, but I can't bring myself to do it now. I scroll back up to the top of the page to log out of his account.

I'll have to get back on this page and screenshot everything going as far back as the bank keeps records. I need to know when it started and how much he actually spent on these women.

I start feeling sick to my stomach, but just as I'm moving my hand toward the mouse pad to click away from the screen, I see another entry.

South Street Medical Clinic, $300.

I frown at the entry. Carlos works in a hospital. He has no reason to go to an obscure medical clinic on the opposite side of town.

There's a second entry four spaces down from the first one.

South Street Medical Clinic, $180.

The entry just below this one is for the same time and the same day as the second clinic visit. This entry reads, *South Street Medical Clinic, Ceftriaxone injection, $100.*

I frown at it trying to figure it out. I don't know what Ceftriaxone is, so I do a Google search on it.

Antibiotic most commonly used in the treatment of gonorrhea.

My throat goes dry. Carlos had gonorrhea. The entry is only two weeks old. I'm on the second page of his bank records.

I can't even blink. This isn't happening. Carlos and I had sex around that time. He better not have given it to me.

I barely remember to log out of his account and shut my computer before I storm out of the suite. I have to find out. I don't know what I'll do if he infected me.

I can't stop squirming inside my skin on my way downstairs. I can't believe I actually have to open my mouth and tell some medical professional about this. This is the worst humiliation yet.

Chapter 13: Holly

The elevator opens in one of the ship's lower decks. The halls all have an industrial look with sterile fluorescent lights, cold, white-grey tile on the floors, and no carpet.

I stop outside the ship's infirmary. It looks like a small hospital. Nurses and a doctor in a white lab coat work in there. I hear them talking about their supplies of drugs, bandages, and splinting equipment.

I can't go in there. I can't go through with this. I can't face the shame even though I have nothing to be ashamed of.

The staff walk back and forth opening cupboards and cabinets while they talk. The doctor is a young guy with curly brown hair. He spots me standing outside in the hall.

He frowns at me and stops what he's doing to come over to me. The name on his lab coat reads, *Dr. Cameron McKinlay, Emergency Medicine.*

"Can I help you with something?" he asks. "Do you need help? Is anything wrong?"

"Um....." I look around at everything other than him. "I'm not sure."

He softens his tone instantly when he sees me shuffling my feet and fidgeting. "Why don't you tell me why you came down here?"

"I....uh......I found out.....a few days ago.....that my husband was cheating on me......He cheated with a lot of people....."

"I'm sorry to hear that. Are you okay?"

"I don't know......" I blurt out. "I just found out he got treated for gonorrhea.....I need to find out if he infected me...."

Dr. McKinlay's expression clears immediately. "Oh, I see. Come on inside and take a seat."

He steers me inside by my elbow and directs me to sit on one of the exam tables. I can't stop knitting my fingers together in agitation.

He crosses the room and comes back with a clipboard. "We'll just need to get your name, all your personal details, and your medical history before we get started. We'll need to do a Pap smear on you, so either I can do it or one of the female nurses can do it if you feel more comfortable with that."

"Um.....I need you to check and see....my husband and I....we've been trying to conceive. I need you to check and see if this is the reason why I couldn't get pregnant."

He only nods. "Of course. That makes perfect sense. Fill out your paperwork and we'll get started. Would you rather get a Pap smear from me or one of the nurses?"

I shrug. "I don't really care."

"Okay. You take care of that and we'll get you all squared away. I want you to know that the treatment for gonorrhea is really simple and straightforward. It's a one-time injection of antibiotics and then a waiting period before you're all clear and infection free. The infection is easily treatable. You're going to be fine even if you are infected."

"But....but it if it did cause infertility.....that could be permanent, couldn't it?"

He tightens his lips. "Yes, it could be, but we don't know if that's the case. Let's take it one step at a time."

He leaves me alone with the clipboard. I fill it out as quickly as I can. Then he comes back, pulls the curtain around my exam table, tells me take off my pants, and to stretch out with the blanket over my lower body.

I shut my brain down while he does the Pap smear. I've gotten so many that they don't mean anything to me anymore.

He tells me I can sit up and get dressed. "You can go back to your own business and I'll call you later with the results."

"I.....I would really rather wait. I don't want to do anything else until I find out."

"I understand. Why don't you come over here and sit in my office?"

He leads me to his office. It's really nice and totally empty.

He sits me on one of the chairs and shuts the door while he goes back out to run the smear results. Thank the stars I got a doctor as nice as he is. He understands perfectly.

He comes back an hour later and sits down opposite me behind his desk. "The test came back positive. You are infected with gonorrhea."

I bury my face in my hands. "I knew it."

"We need to run some more thorough tests to check whether the infection is impacting your fertility. We'll take a blood sample to check your hormone levels and then we'll need to do an ultrasound of your uterus. The infection could be causing low-level inflammation of your uterine lining that's stopping you from getting pregnant."

I take my hands down and lock eyes on him. "Tell me the truth. The inflammation could be so severe that it's permanent. Don't sugar-coat it."

"There are times when the inflammation can get so severe that it causes scarring to the inner surface of your uterus," he tells me. "Those cases usually involved long-term exposure, so it really depends on how long you've been carrying the infection. Do you have any idea how long ago your husband might have exposed you?"

"The records I found were only from three weeks ago, but he could have infected me long before that. He could have gotten it years ago."

He spreads his hands. "Then we better do the ultrasound and find out. Any scar tissue will show up on the scans. Then at least you'll know what you're dealing with."

He takes me back out to the infirmary, does a quick blood draw, and hands the sample off to one of the nurses to run the tests on my hormone levels.

Then he tells me to lie down on the exam table again and to pull up my shirt.

He squirts ice-cold gel on my stomach and switches on the machine. I can't see anything on there. He rotates the wand all the way down to my pubic bone and deeper into my pelvis.

"Okay, here we go," he murmurs. "Ah, yes. The inner surface of your uterus is inflamed. That lining is showing up nice and clear. That explains why you aren't able to get pregnant......I don't see any scar tissue....."

He goes through the rest of the scan. He rotates the wand back and forth in all directions.

"I don't see any scarring. It looks like your uterus is still in good shape. You should be able to conceive as soon as the infection clears."

"So....can I get the injection now?" I ask.

"Yes. Get dressed and let me check your blood hormone levels. Then we'll give you the injection."

He leaves while I wipe the gel off my stomach and sit up. I go through the rest of the visit in a whirlwind of emotions.

The doctor tells me all my hormone levels check out. There's nothing wrong with me. Then he gives me an injection in the top of my buttocks and tells me I'm still contagious for another week.

I can barely think straight by the time I leave the infirmary. I don't know how to cope with all this information bursting out of my head.

I'm not infertile. Carlos infected me with gonorrhea. That's why I couldn't get pregnant.

What a lowlife bastard scumbag he is. How could he do this to me—and then have the nerve to blame me for not being able to get pregnant?

I have to remind myself that he never wanted to get pregnant. Did he do this on purpose?

He couldn't have. He's a brainless cheater. He doesn't care about anything other than sticking his pecker into any warm hole that happens to cross his path.

I can't believe I was actually one of those women. Who else did he give it to?

I storm out of the elevator on my way back to my suite, turn a corner, and collide with Nate. "Whoa!" he exclaims. "Where's the fire?"

I barely look at him, step around him, and walk away as fast as I can. "I can't talk to you right now, Nate. I gotta go."

"Hey!" He follows me. "What's going on? Hey! Talk to me! Are we still on for dinner tonight?"

"Leave me alone!" I snap over my shoulder. "I can't talk to you right now!"

"Should I come and get you at seven or not? Just tell me that much. A simple yes or no will do."

"No!" I snap.

"Will you at least tell me why? Did I do something to piss you off? I didn't mean to."

I spin around too fast. "Carlos infected me with gonorrhea, Nate! Are you happy now? I just found out and now I have a low-level infection in my uterus that is stopping me from getting pregnant. Okay? My skank husband infected me with a disease."

He stands there with his mouth hanging open in horror. "Oh, my God! I am so sorry, sweetie!"

I throw up my hands and turn away, but I can't leave now. He already knows the worst. "You talking about your brother finding that footage made me look into Carlos's affairs. I just found all his bank records going back for years. That's how I found out."

He wilts in defeat. "I'm so sorry. We don't have to go out to dinner. I understand. I'll leave you alone."

"No! You don't have to leave. I just.....I don't know what to do with all of this."

"Do you want to go for a walk? We could go to the observation deck at the end of the hall. You don't have to be alone."

I nod and blunder down the hall in a trance. My brain doesn't want to function.

He opens the doors to the observation deck and we step outside. I go out to the railing and turn my face into the salty breeze.

He sits down on a bench behind me. He doesn't say anything. He just sits there.

I'm glad he's here, now that I get over my initial reluctance to tell him the truth. He knows. Someone knows and I'm glad it's him.

I'm going to be okay. I'm still fertile, but knowing that doesn't help at all.

The sun is sinking toward the horizon. It's getting late. I should go inside, but I don't seem to be able to do anything.

I don't know what to do with any part of my life. I don't seem to be able to go forward or backward.

I turn back to go inside, but I can't walk away from Nate. I sit down next to him and he touches my arm once. That's all.

"Do you still want to go out to dinner tonight?" he asks. "We don't have to. We could just sit in a quiet place while you process all of this."

"I don't know what I want to do," I mumble. "I don't know how to do any of this."

"You don't have to. This is so much worse than we thought. You don't have to cope."

"I guess I have no reason not to go out. I'm just worried I wouldn't be very good company for you tonight. I'm not in the mood for witty banter."

"We don't have to do witty banter. We can sit there in silence if you need to."

I look away. "How did this happen?"

"It happened because he lied to you. That's how it happened. You have to remember that none of this is your fault. Trusting your husband doesn't make you stupid or gullible. You had every reason to believe you could trust him. He's the asshole here, not you."

"How would I know I have what it takes to choose someone better? I thought he was a good person. If he could trick me, how do I know the next person won't do the same thing?"

"I'm sure you're smart enough to know, especially since you'll be on the lookout for it from now on. Not every man is as much of a dirtbag as he is. His kind give the rest of us a bad name, but we aren't all like that."

I do my best to smile at him. "I know you aren't."

He touches my arm again. "We can do whatever you want to do tonight—or we don't have to do anything. You can go back to your suite and survive on room service."

I snort. "That's exactly what I can't do. I should go out. I don't want my life to fall apart because of this."

"So.....do you want to go inside now....or we could stay out here."

"It's getting late. I should probably go get ready."

"Okay." He walks me inside and we part at my door. "I'll see you at seven."

Chapter 14: Nate

I knock on Holly's door and she answers it wearing a very conservative black dress. It has a high scoop neck, long sleeves, and no frills.

She wears minimal jewelry and no other accessories. I see at a glance that she doesn't want to give anyone any ideas about her availability.

I get the message loud and clear. She wants to put up her walls to protect herself. I don't blame her after everything that's been happening.

I don't offer her my arm or put her hand on my arm or anything like that. We barely talk and keep it superficial as I escort her downstairs.

We settle into a different restaurant. This one is less fancy. Sitting across from her doesn't feel as much like we're on a date.

She looks and dresses like she's in mourning—which I suppose she is. She's the widow. I'm just a supportive friend taking her out to dinner.

I order a bottle of wine and pour her a glass. I raise mine in a toast to her. "Here's to you. You're going to come through this and conquer. I know you will."

She snorts. "You could have hit me over the head with a croquet mallet when I found out."

I wind up laughing. "Sorry. I know it isn't funny."

Her lips twitch. "That's okay. I guess I was kinda hoping you would."

"Hey, you can hit me over the head with a croquet mallet if it makes you feel better."

She bursts out laughing. "You're such a trooper."

"Anything for you. Just make sure you do it close to some medical facility so they can treat me for the traumatic brain injury I'm going to sustain."

She starts laughing again—but her smile vanishes the way it did the other night. I follow her gaze to Carlos and Alexis.

They're in a different restaurant this time. She spots them through the windows of both establishments. They don't know we're here.

She narrows her eyes at them and then stands up so fast she knocks her chair over. "I can't do this! I'm sorry, Nate!"

She jerks back and forth in confusion trying to decide if she should pick up her chair before she rushes out of the restaurant. She leaves the chair lying there.

I scramble to pick it up, apologize profusely to the restaurant staff, and go after her.

I catch up with her in the breezeway next to the piazza. She paces up and down wiping her hand across her forehead and grimacing in misery.

"Hey!" I tell her. "No big deal! You don't have to go out there."

"He could be out there infecting half the population!" she blurts out. "He could be infecting Alexis right now! He did it with me while he was infected. Then he got treated and did it with me again without telling me that he ever had it! I could have reinfected him! He could be walking around with it right now!"

I step in next to her and walk up and down the deck next to her. She just needs to rant and that's okay.

"He could have contracted it from one person and spread it to hundreds of others! He's the walking equivalent of the Black Plague! The people who treated him must have told him to inform all his sexual partners—but he didn't—because he didn't tell me!"

"Did you find anything else in his bank records?" I ask.

"He was spending hundreds and probably thousands of dollars on expensive jewelry, lingerie, flowers, and gifts for other women. He never bought anything like that for me! He never even mentioned buying me jewelry until we came on this cruise."

"It sounds like he was living out his fantasies with them."

"He was living out his fantasies by spreading sexually transmitted diseases far and wide across the countryside!" She snorts. "This is the piece of trash I married and dedicated my life to."

We come to the end of the breezeway. She continues to the rear deck. Only a faint glow of light makes it out this far from the rooms inside the piazza and the concourse.

She stops at the railing. The moon casts a silver glow on the ship's wake. The wind feels cooler now than it did during the day.

"You should go inside," I tell her. "I don't want you to get cold."

She barely hears me. "Why am I even here? I should just leave. Seeing them together is only going to upset me."

"My brother told me I should come home, but I said I wasn't ready to do that yet."

"This is stupid," she mumbles. "I really need to snap out of it."

I turn to face her in the moonlight. She doesn't turn to face me until I take her hand and turn her around.

I look deep into her eyes. I want her to understand exactly what I mean. "I stayed because of you. What we're sharing right now means so much to me. I didn't want it to end prematurely."

I cup her cheeks and lean in to kiss her. This has been coming for a long time—or as long as the two of us have been single.

I don't want this to end. I don't want to spend any time on this cruise away from her.

She pulls away and shakes my hands off her face. "I can't do that, Nate. I'm sorry."

"You don't have to. I just want you to know how I feel about you."

"I can't do anything until I get a clean bill of health—and I don't know if I could do anything with you or not. I like you a lot, but I want children and a family. I don't want to get involved with anyone unless it's serious—like forever."

"I understand," I tell her.

"You understand, but you aren't there yourself. You're too uncertain about your future and if you even want a family anymore. You keep saying this whole thing with Alexis is making you question if you really want that." She shakes her head again. "I like you a lot, but I don't think you're what I'm looking for. Thank you again for tonight. I better go."

She hurries away and leaves me standing there with my head in a whirl. Did that just happen?

I know she likes me. She probably even likes me in that way.

I kissed her. I would like to have a whirlwind fling with her just to pay Carlos and Alexis back for their betrayal.

That is the absolute worst thing I could do to Holly. She's too good to go through with something like that.

I would only insult her again by suggesting it. Is that why I kissed her—to get back at Carlos and Alexis? Did I already insult her by trying to take our friendship to the next level?

I kick myself for that. She's too good for anyone to treat her as a fly-by-night convenience. She's too precious.

I should have treated her better, especially since I already knew she only wanted something serious.

I go upstairs to my suite and change into my pajamas, but I can't sleep. I go out to my balcony where I can see the ocean and the stars.

I want something serious, too. I want a family. I always have wanted one.

I thought Alexis was going to be the one. That simple desire to be a husband and a father didn't go away when I found out about her cheating.

This whole thing about turning my back on it and going rootless—that was all a reaction to this situation. It isn't really how I feel. I don't really want to be rootless.

My brothers are all married. I'm the only one left out in the cold. I always planned to change that with the right woman.

Don't ask me why I thought Alexis would make a good mother. Maybe it's her whole 1950s housewife vibe, but her personality couldn't be further from what I consider a good mother.

Holly wants children more than anything. She must have been dreaming about it for years. She's fun-loving and smart. She's a home-loving person with a flexible job.

She's also loyal. She gave Carlos everything. She would do the same thing for any man she married and built a family with.

What could be better than that?

Chapter 15: Holly

I stroll along the concourse window shopping in all the stores. I don't plan to buy anything. I just want to kill some time and take my mind off of everything serious in my life.

I'm just passing the electronics store when Nate comes out of it holding a box and squinting at his receipt.

"Good morning," he tells me when he sees me. "Good to see you out and about in daylight. The blood of the Day Walker is strong in you."

I snort with laughter. "Nice one. What did you buy?"

He waves the box at me. "It's a Bluetooth mouse for my laptop. I stayed up way too late working on the computer last night and pulled a muscle in my wrist working on the trackpad mouse."

"Oh, no," I tease. "Do you need one of those orthopedic wrist braces?"

He nods. "I was thinking about getting one next. Are you busy? Do you want to come?"

"Okay. Why not?"

We stroll down the concourse. I hang out cruising the aisles of the drug store while he picks out the brace he wants. The clerk even lets him try it on to make sure it fits.

He leaves the brace on when we leave. "Why did you stay up so late last night?" I ask.

"Actually, if you really want to know the truth, I stayed up all night. I couldn't sleep, so I wound up staying up until dawn. I'll probably crash later."

"Why? I hope you weren't too upset about our conversation."

He takes hold of my arm, pulls me to a stop, and turns me around to face him. "Listen to me, sweetie. I wasn't upset about our conversation—because you were absolutely right about me. I wasn't serious—which is stupid because I do want a family. I was just having a reaction to this whole Alexis breakup—but you're right. I do want that—and I want to do better for you. I know what you said last night, but I really think we have a chance here. You're like no one I've ever met. I want to prove myself to you if you just give me a chance. I don't want me not being serious to be the reason you decide against me—because I am serious. I want a family and I really want you to be the one. I think it could work out really well. What do you say?"

I stare up at him for a second trying to take all of that in, but I shake it off just as fast. "I really like you, Nate. I have a really good feeling about you, but we're only on this cruise for a little while. We live on opposite sides of the state. We probably won't see each other again after this. We shouldn't get serious about each other. Besides, I can't do anything until I finish the antibiotics...."

"I don't care about that," he blurts out. "We can keep it strictly platonic until then. We can at least keep spending time together and supporting each other. Right?"

I can't help but smile at him. "Right."

"Come have lunch with me." He waves his mouse box over his shoulder. "Let me just go upstairs and put this in my suite. Do you want to come? I can meet you back down here if you don't."

"I'll come. I have nothing else to do."

We set off for the piazza and the elevators. "What were you working on last night while you were burning the midnight oil?" I ask.

"I had a lot on my mind after we talked on the deck. I thought it over and decided that, yes, I do want to find someone serious even if it isn't with you."

"Tell me you didn't sign up for a bunch of dating sites."

He laughs and his eyes twinkle at me. "Something tells me I wouldn't find what I'm looking for there. Anyway, no, I didn't sign up for the dating sites. I went on my company website and looked for jobs that don't require traveling. Then I searched the whole state and found some listings that look promising. I need to update my resume and start thinking about settling down in one particular place."

"But won't that depend on where meet someone? You might meet someone online and have to relocate to settle closer to them."

"I decided to definitely stay in the Seattle area. My family is there and I don't want to move away. I also have my house—which would be perfect for a family. I don't want to lose ground. I just need to find the right person."

"Wow," I exclaim. "You really accomplished a lot in one night."

"Talking to you clarified a lot of things in my mind—so I'm grateful to you for that. I realized it isn't so much about you. It's about me and what I really want out of life. All that stuff about becoming a wandering salesman and forgetting about family—that isn't me. That was just the breakup talking—and something else you said really stuck out at me, too."

"Did it hit you over the head with a croquet mallet?"

He laughs again. He actually looks happier and more relaxed than he has since the breakup.

"You could say it was something like that," he replies. "You said it never works to go on the dating market without knowing exactly what you want. You said you would have to be upfront with everyone about what you were looking for and that would eliminate ninety-eight percent of the dating pool."

I grimace. "Yeah. That's one of the reasons I don't want to do it."

"But don't you see? That's exactly what we have to do. We have to put it all out there. Eliminating all those people will reduce the pool to only the qualified candidates. That will actually make it a thousand times easier to find the right person. We won't have to wade through all these other pretenders."

I cock my head to one side. "That's interesting. I didn't think of it that way, but you're right."

He stops in front of his suite door, unlocks it, and sticks the mouse box inside before he comes back out. "Anyway, I just couldn't shut my brain off last night. I couldn't stop thinking about it once I started, so I just kept going—but in a good way. The whole thing energized me—like I couldn't wait to get started. I was busting with it."

He laughs again, but right at that moment, we turn a corner and see Carlos coming out of another suite. It isn't the suite he shares with Alexis.

He steps out into the hall with his back to us. He doesn't see me and Nate standing right there watching him.

A woman in a short, skimpy robe follows him as far as the threshold. Her blonde hair is a mess and so is her makeup.

She puts her arms around him, gives him a sloppy kiss with all her smeared lipstick, and undulates her body against him. She looks like someone just rolled her in the gutter.

I stare at them as the truth sinks in. He must have just screwed her in her suite. Is she married? I'll probably never know.

He sticks his tongue down her throat and even grabs her ass under her too-short robe. That robe doesn't hide anything.

She moans—and like it was meant to be, Alexis comes around the corner right at that moment.

She stops in her tracks when she sees Carlos with this other woman. The woman doesn't notice anything out of the ordinary. She has her face so glued to Carlos's that neither of them sees a thing until it's too late.

He finally pulls away, leers at the woman, gives her a swat on the backside, and says, "I'll catch up with you later, okay?"

She smirks, runs her tongue over her smeared lips, and gives him a smoky look as she pulls away. "You better," she husks.

He smiles. He doesn't know he has lipstick all over his face. God, he looks like such a sleaze.

Alexis jolts out of her trance and storms up to both of them. "What the hell do you think you're doing?!" She yanks Carlos away from the woman. "You get your hands off him! He's mine!"

The woman looks down her nose at Alexis. "You aren't doing a very good job of keeping him. Try harder and you might have better success pleasing a man."

"You bitch!" Alexis snaps. "You stay away from him!"

"What are you—his wife?" The woman scoffs in Alexis's face. "Good luck keeping a hot-blooded lover like this."

The woman gives Carlos another seductive look—or what she probably hopes is a seductive look.

"Actually, I'm his wife," I call over.

They all spin around to stare at me.

I point at Alexis. "This tramp stole him from me—and you all might be really happy to know that he's infected with gonorrhea. He probably already gave it to you—and any of the other hundreds of women he slept with while he was infected. Have a nice day."

Alexis and the other woman turn on Carlos in a rage. They both start yelling at him. He has to yell back to make himself heard.

Alexis points at me, yells, and I see her winding up to confront me next. I take a step forward, but Nate pulls me away to stop me from going over there.

He tugs me farther backward, but before we can leave, the woman strikes out and slaps Carlos hard across the face.

He spins around and Alexis punches him in the stomach. They both start whaling on him from both directions. He cowers under his arms, and right then, the elevator opens and a squad of security guards emerge into the hall.

They surround the combatants, pull everyone apart, and separate Carlos from the other two women so they can't get to them.

Nate pulls my arm one more time. "Let's get out of here before this gets any worse."

Chapter 16: Nate

I climb out of the pool, shake the water out of my hair, and head over to where I left my towel and phone. I rub my hair dry and sit down on a nearby deck chair to put my shoes on before I go back up to my suite to change.

Holly has a doctor's appointment today to find out how much the antibiotics are improving the infection in her uterus. I won't see her until this afternoon.

I want to get upstairs so I can start applying for some of these local jobs. I also need to do some web research on how I can meet up with eligible women who want to start families.

Maybe I should talk to my parents—or join a church—or something like that. Holly is right. The online dating world is a sewer. I don't want to go that route.

I pull on my shirt and pick up my phone and damp towel, but before I can stand up, Alexis sits down on the lounge chair next to me.

She's already crying hard and she sobs openly the minute she sits down.

"What do you want?" I snap. "Haven't you done enough damage to my life already?"

"I have gonorrhea, Nate!" she wails. "Carlos gave it to me—and now four other women on the ship are coming forward to say he gave it to them, too!"

I snort at her. "Good. You got exactly what you deserved. I hope you're happy."

"I didn't mean to hurt you!" she chokes. "I was lonely at home by myself the whole time! You can't blame me for that!"

"There's a big difference between you being lonely at home by yourself and turning my house into Grand Central Station with hundreds of different guys coming through one after the other to use your body and move along to make room for the next guy."

"It was never like that!" she howls.

"It was very much like that. I got video evidence of all the guys coming over while I was out of town. Don't even waste your breath trying to deny it. I just hope you made some decent money off it."

"Nate!" she screams. "How can you even say that?!"

"I'm just telling it like it is. At least maybe then you would have something to show for it because you won't get a penny from the divorce."

"Divorce?!" she counters. "Give me another chance!"

"Why should I—so you can give me gonorrhea? I will never lay a finger on you again—and you sure as hell won't ever come to my house again—not even as a guest."

"I'm sorry!" she bawls. "I made a mistake! Can't you forgive me?"

"No," I snap. "I will never forgive you. I'll pack up your stuff and leave the boxes out on the front lawn. You can come and get them. You won't come inside. You ruined my life and Holly's life. Did you know this gonorrhea is the reason she couldn't get pregnant? Did you know you could be doing that to God only knows how many other women? That is unforgivable to me, so don't ever come crawling to me again asking for another chance. You killed our marriage. Now you get to live with it."

I stand up, walk off, and leave her there crying into her hands. The stupid cow isn't crying for me or Holly or any of the other loyal, unsuspecting wives Alexis might have hurt.

She's only crying for herself. She only cares about any of this because the consequences came back to bite her in the ass—literally.

Good. I'm glad she's upset. I'm glad she's hurting. I'm glad she finally feels that she might have made a mistake.

I don't hold out much hope that she'll learn from this, but Alexis is someone else's problem now. She's her own problem that only she can fix.

I go upstairs and change my clothes. I'm just getting ready to sit down at the computer when I get a text from Holly.

I'm done. What are you doing? Do you want to meet up?

I text her back and head down to the piazza to find her.

"Did you just come up from the infirmary?" I ask. "I thought I wouldn't see you until later."

"Not quite. I just saw Carlos. He came weaseling back asking for another chance."

I laugh. "Really? Alexis just did the same thing. She has gonorrhea—and so do a bunch of other women on the ship."

She makes a face at me. "He's under investigation by the cruise line security team. He might get thrown off the cruise for knowingly endangering these women when he knew he had a transmissible disease."

"Wow. That's really bad."

"I still don't think he even understands how bad it is that he nearly made me permanently infertile by not telling me. He just doesn't grasp that it could be that important to me."

"We already knew he was a selfish clueless idiot. It's interesting. I just had the same thought about Alexis. She doesn't care about any of this except how it affects her. She doesn't even think about all the lives and marriages she's ruining."

"I told him I hope he does get thrown off the ship," she goes on. "I told him to move out of the house and be gone by the time I get home."

"Dang. Harsh."

She laughs—and then slips her arm through mine. "So what are we going to do to celebrate?"

I become aware of her standing too close to me. This is definitely not a platonic, friendly hold.

"What are we celebrating?" I ask. "You don't get the all-clear for another three days."

She blushes at me. Did I just actually suggest that?

"I don't know what we're celebrating," she replies. "Unless it's finally putting those two rats behind us. I just feel like celebrating. Come on."

She pulls me into the concourse and enters one of the bars. "Now I'm worried," I tell her. "It isn't even three o'clock in the afternoon, you know."

She laughs again. Her eyes sparkle and she won't stop blushing. "I was going to get something non-alcoholic, but feel free to tie one on. I'll make sure you get home safely."

"Are you sure? Maybe I should be worried about you taking advantage of me in my inebriated state."

She bursts out laughing and stops at the bar. She orders a Shirley Temple. I get a Virgin Mary.

We sit opposite each other on high stools at a table in the middle of the bar. She taps her glass against mine. "Here's to new beginnings and putting the past behind us."

We both sip our drinks. "I'm going to assume the antibiotics are working."

She nods. "The infection is going down. Dr. McKinlay actually suggested that I go on some kind of birth control, but I told him I'm not ready to start doing it with anyone else just yet. I told him I would go on it when I was ready for that."

"So...." I let my eyes trail down to her body. "So you're like a walking timebomb ready to blow."

She laughs and blushes again. "You would have to get a lot closer than that for me to blow up."

Am I seeing a meaningful sparkle in her eyes—or am I just imagining it? She acts a lot more intimate toward me than she ever has before.

She keeps shooting me flirtatious little smirks over her drink. I become aware of her lips closing around her straw when she takes a sip.

I could be reading too much into this, but it sure looks like she's trying to send me a signal. Is she finally opening up to the idea that something could happen between us?

Should I take that chance if we're only going to go our separate ways at the end of the cruise?

I have to find out if there is even a chance. She would be my very first choice of a woman to get together and lock myself down with. I can't think of anyone better.

I have to try it at least to find out if there is a chance.

We finish our drinks and head down the concourse in no particular direction. "Are you going to go shopping to celebrate now?" I ask.

She smirks at me again and leads me over to the jewelry store. "I could buy myself all the expensive jewelry Carlos bought for his many women. I could treat myself to all the jewelry he never bought for me."

"I could buy you something," I blurt out.

She spins around and her mouth falls open. "No, you couldn't! I couldn't let you do that!"

"What about one of those?" I point to the diamond engagement rings in the case.

She gapes at them and then her cheeks turn bright red before she turns away. I trail after her, but I don't restart the conversation. There. Two can play this little game.

We stop by the theaters and show halls next. We look at all the playbills to see what shows are playing.

"Avery Girbach is playing tonight," she suggests. "We could go see that."

"That doesn't start until eight-thirty tonight. Would you like to have dinner with me beforehand?"

I say it in that way that makes it obvious I'm asking her out. This isn't a friendly invitation.

She blushes at me and slips her hand into mine. She clasps it in a very non-friendly way. "I would love to. Thank you. I always like going out with you."

I lead her back toward the piazza. "Think about what I said," I tell her.

She frowns. "What you said about what?"

"About the ring. I would really like to give you one, but I don't want to put any pressure on you. Just think about it. Think about me—in that way—if you want to."

She looks away. We're still holding hands when we step into the elevator. Other people get in with us. No one notices or cares that we're holding hands. They all think we're a couple.

We're still holding hands when we stop in front of her suite. She beams up at me. "Thank you."

"For what?" I ask.

"For everything. I....I really like you."

"Stop saying that. That's like the worst thing you can say to a guy."

She laughs. "Would you rather I said I didn't like you?"

"Just tell me you'll think about it."

"I am thinking about it."

My eyebrows shoot up. "You are?"

"Of course! How could I not think about it when you're always there for me and always make everything better? Who else would I be thinking about?"

"Oh." I frown. "I didn't know you were thinking about it. I thought you made up your mind that I was off the table."

She smiles at me. It's such a warm, accepting smile. "You are on the table."

I throw caution to the wind and kiss her. She's basically been inviting me to do it ever since we met up today.

She kisses me back—and our lips lock together. My arms glide around her back and I lift her against me.

Her kisses escalate with mine. We kiss faster and harder. I want to grab her and crush her, but I don't want to push her too far.

She's really kissing me back. She doesn't pull away. She matches me exactly when her tongue meets mine and she turns her head sideways to sink all the way into my mouth.

I drown in that feeling of blissful warmth, peace, and softness. Holy crap, she feels so good! She feels so much better than I ever let myself hope.

I'm on the table. She actually said that—and now she's kissing me and running her fingers through my hair and letting me rock her in my arms. I never want to stop. I never want to let her go.

I have to let her go, though. She eases back, gives me a dozen more light, delicious, sensual little kisses, and I put her feet back down on the floor before I straighten up.

"I'll see you tonight," she murmurs. "Seven o'clock as usual?"

"We should leave earlier if we want to get dinner before the show. I'll come around six."

She blushes and smiles at me. "Okay. I'll see you then."

Chapter 17: Nate

I check my watch for the hundredth time. Holly is downstairs having another checkup with the medical team.

She should be getting clearance today that she's disease free. I don't know what's going to happen if she is.

We've been kissing, holding hands, and looking into each other's eyes for three days. It sure feels like love—or maybe just the beginnings of it.

She doesn't say if she'll go on some kind of birth control after this and I don't ask. Maybe she's downstairs talking to the doctors and nurses about that right this minute.

I just have to wait to hear what she wants to do.

I really wouldn't care if she decided not to have sex again until after she gets married. I would marry her right now without ever having sex with her.

I would already have proposed to her if I thought I stood a snowball's chance in Hell of her accepting.

I don't want to step on her toes. She already knows how I feel. I just have to wait for her to be ready.

I can wait until doomsday if I have to. I would go to any lengths if I thought I had a prayer of marrying her.

I pace up and down the concourse not seeing anything. I just have to keep myself occupied until she gets back.

I can't stop my mind from racing. Pacing around the concourse also brings me past the jewelry store window again and again. I can't help but see all the engagement rings and wedding bands on display.

She's so special. I love everything about her. Yes, I really did think that. She's my cornerstone. I don't care where I go after this or what happens as long as we stay together.

I'm on the table. She said so. That's more than I hoped. Maybe, just maybe it can grow into more than that.

I head over to the theaters again to check out the playbills. They haven't changed since I came over here to read them ten minutes ago, but I have to do something with the extra time.

I get halfway across the concourse when Carlos shoves his way through the surrounding shoppers. He stops in front of me and gets in my face. "What's your problem?!" he snaps.

"I don't have a problem, man," I tell him. "Except for you. You're the only problem here."

"You stole my wife right out from under me!" He points in my face. "Don't think I don't see you walking around holding hands with her! You stay away from her."

I snort in his face. *"You* stole your wife right out from under you, pal. She loved you with all her heart and soul. She stayed loyal to you for years, but we can't say the same thing about you, can we? You're too stupid for a woman like that. She was bound to get with another man eventually. I just got lucky enough to be here to help her through it when you betrayed her and ruined her life. So thanks. I owe you a big one for that."

I clap him on the shoulder and step forward to walk past him. I don't have time to deal with this piece of dog shit on the bottom of my shoe.

He spins around and throws a punch at me. I dodge in time and he stumbles. A bunch of nearby shoppers scream and back away just as a bunch of security guards roll out of the nearest bar.

They grab Carlos and pull him away from me. Troy Nixon steps in and blocks Carlos from me.

Troy has to yell to make himself heard over Carlos's enraged bellows. "You're banned from the ship, Mr. Silverman!" Troy announces. "I saw you assault this man unprovoked—and I also have evidence that you knowingly infected four different women on the cruise with gonorrhea when you knew you were still contagious. This is a violation of the Paradise Cruise Lines' health and safety policies. You'll be removed from the ship and extradited back to the US within the next twenty-four hours."

The guards march Carlos away. He struggles and they have to yank him by the jacket to keep him on his feet.

Troy makes one instant of eye contact with me before he walks away. He leaves me standing there stunned. It's over—for Carlos, at least.

I wander off in a daze. I have to tell Holly about this, and ten minutes later, I get a text from here.

I'm done and I'm on my way up to the piazza right now. See you there?

I text back. *Hell yes.*

She doesn't respond. I go to the piazza and wait for her by the elevators. She steps out looking calm and thoughtful.

I take her hand, but I can't read her. "How did it go?"

She pulls me onto the rear deck, pushes me against the wall, and attacks me kissing me like crazy. I have to race to keep up with her.

She presses her whole body against me in a passionate embrace. She kisses me hard and fast, rubs my neck, and even strokes my cheeks while I kiss her back.

She finally settles down and sinks onto her feet to look up at me. "Does that mean you're all clear?" I ask.

She bursts out in excited giggles. "Yeah!"

I clasp her hand. "That's wonderful! Congratulations! I'm so happy for you.....I have some other news for you."

Her smile drains. "What is it? Is it something bad?"

"Not at all. Carlos is getting thrown off the ship."

She gasps out loud. "No way!"

"He just threw a punch at me on the concourse. Troy and a bunch of other guards were standing right there and saw him—and Troy has confirmation that he infected four other women on the ship—including Alexis. Carlos is a danger to everyone. He's out."

"Wow!" She passes her hand across her forehead. "I never believed it would actually happen."

I take her hand again. "So...do you want to go on a real date with me tonight—now that you're finally free?"

She laughs again. She giggles like a kid in a candy store. "Yeah! Let's do it!"

"Great. I'll see you at your place at seven."

Chapter 18: Holly

I open my door and find Nate standing there waiting for me. I grab his hand and pull him inside so I can kiss him again before we go downstairs for dinner.

I love kissing him. I love being near him. I'm really starting to love everything about the guy.

He's so considerate and attentive and supportive. I don't see how I can separate from him after this cruise.

His comments implying that we would get married—I really can't see any better outcome than that.

We both like and respect each other. We both want the same things. We both know the other one is loyal, caring, and committed to this.

I don't see how I can build any stronger foundation with someone else. Where would I even begin to look?

Looking somewhere else is the last thing in the world I want to do. Why should I when I have the most perfect man right here in front of me?

He finally pulls back. "We'll miss our reservation if we don't go now—or we can stay here and get room service."

I laugh and feel myself blushing. "Let's save that for the honeymoon."

His eyes go hard when he understands what I mean. "Let's go. We can talk about that later."

He leads me downstairs. The restaurant he takes me to is one of the nicer ones on the ship. It's also way busier than he expected.

"I'm not so sure about this!" he yells over the noise while we wait to be seated. "Maybe we should go somewhere else!"

"It's Friday night!" I yell back. "Everywhere will be busy! We're already here and you have a reservation! Let's just ride it out!"

We do and it pays off. We're one of the first parties to get a table. We sit down and the waiter leaves our bottle of wine and our menus.

A large group of what looks like businessmen crowds over near the bar. "It looks like most of those people waiting didn't make reservations!" I point out.

"Stick with me," he replies. "I'll never let you go hungry."

I smile at him, but all of this noise makes it difficult to talk. That doesn't stop us from gazing at each other across the table. I can't deny that he is definitely acting romantic.

He touches his wine glass to mine and leans across the table to say, "Congratulations," into my ear.

His breath on my ear and neck gives me tingles. We've been acting so intimate for the last few days.

Now I'm disease free. I feel like I should go out and sleep with someone just because I can.

I don't want to do that. Dr. McKinlay mentioned again today that I should be on birth control because I can get pregnant anytime now.

I don't want to sleep with someone. I mean, I want to sleep with someone, but not just anyone. I want to sleep with Nate. Should I?

I don't want to do that unless things are going to materialize between us. He certainly seems to want that.

I want it, too. That's the truth. I want to get together with him, but the idea of taking that leap scares the crap out of me.

I didn't realize until now that it does scare me. I really wanted to have children with Carlos, but maybe I wanted it so badly because I couldn't. Maybe I didn't realize before just exactly what I was signing up for.

Nate extends his hand across the table and I take it. We just sit here holding hands, drinking our wine, and appreciating each other's company. We can talk after this and I know we will. We'll talk about everything. I have no secrets from this man.

Just then, we hear a commotion behind our table—or behind Nate. I'm already facing that way.

Troy and a bunch of his security guards elbow their way into the group of businessmen. I hear Troy yelling, "Excuse me! Excuse me! Security! Open up! Back off, Mister! Security! Excuse me! Let me through, please!"

The businessmen pull back to let the guards through. Nate goes deadly still when we see Alexis over there in the middle of the crowd.

She's dressed up to the nines with a super low-cut dress that lets all her cleavage spill out. The slit up the side of her skirt exposes her thigh almost to the hip.

She's in the middle of laughing loudly at the men around her. They stand extra close to her and stare into her face from all sides. The energy coming from the group blasts across the room.

The men closest to her don't notice anything out of the ordinary until Troy and his men push their way through the crowd and make their way to Alexis.

Everyone else in the whole restaurant notices the commotion. The businessmen fall silent as the security guards break up their gathering.

The noise in the place dwindles to nothing until we can only hear Alexis talking to the three or four men nearest her.

Troy pulls up next to her. She's so smitten with the men around her that she doesn't notice him until he takes hold of her elbow. "Come with me, please, Ms. Whitman."

"Hey!" She spins around and tries to pull her away from him. "Leave me alone! I didn't do anything wrong!"

"We already talked about this, Ma'am...." he tells her.

"Leave her alone, man!" one of the businessmen interjects. "What's the problem?"

I get a really bad feeling about this when Troy turns around to face all the businessmen. There must be thirty men over there all crowding around trying to hit on Alexis.

"You all might like to know that this woman just tested positive for gonorrhea four days ago," Troy announces to the entire silent restaurant and bar. "She'll still be contagious for another four days before she gets a medical clearance. I already spoke to her more than once and warned her not to sleep with anyone on the ship before then—so I would advise all of you gentlemen to keep your pants zipped and be a little more discerning about who you associate with."

Alexis cringes—as well she might. Nate shoots me a smirk of wild glee. All the businessmen change their expressions real quick. Some even curl their lips at Alexis or just turn their backs on her.

She hunches her shoulders and won't look at anyone when Troy pulls her farther down the bar. Conversation around the room starts back up slowly until the same tide of noise washes through the room.

It drowns out whatever Troy says to Alexis. He stands nose to nose with her and gives her the reprimand of a lifetime right in front of everyone. Damn. That guy certainly knows how to give some no-good scoundrel a smackdown.

She cowers in front of him, rubs her arms, and screws her fancy high heels into the floor. She won't look up at him while he snaps in her face.

He eventually swipes his finger toward the exit and she rushes away. Nate bursts out laughing, squeezes my hand, and raises his wine glass to me. His cheeks won't stop glowing with pleasure.

I can't help but smile back at him. He must feel pretty good about seeing her get what she deserves. I'm happy for him.

The businessmen leave before our food comes. The restaurant quiets down so we can finally talk. "So who do you plan to bed first—now that you're a free agent?" he asks.

I turn bright red. "Stop it. I don't plan to bed anyone."

He raises his wine glass. "Don't let yourself go to waste."

"You don't have gonorrhea and I don't see you bedding anyone."

He laughs. "Let's call it slow progress toward a definite goal." He raises his glass again. "I'm playing the long game."

I try not to show that I know exactly what he's talking about. He can drop hints as well as I can—if not better than I can.

We finally get out of there and wander out onto the moonlit rear deck. We always wind up coming out here for romantic walks in the moonlight.

We hold hands and then he puts his arm around my shoulders. We both might be able to fool ourselves about this being a friendly, platonic hug, but we've both gone way beyond platonic by this time.

I should say something. I should bring up the subject. We should make a decision about whether we're doing this or not.

He pulls me down on one of the benches and puts his arm around me there, too. Now is the time. I can't put it off any longer.

He breaks the silence before I can even say anything. "When are you going to give me an answer about my suggestion?"

I look up. "Suggestion?"

"Come on, sweetheart. You know what I mean. Let's not beat around the bush anymore. You know I want to take this further."

"How much further do you want to take it?"

"I already told you that, too. I put all my cards out on the table. Now it's your turn. Just tell me whether you want to do this with me or not. It isn't complicated. There's no pressure. Just tell me what's going on with you."

"I already told you where I stand, too. I don't want to do it with someone unless it's the real thing—especially since I'm not on any birth control. I could get pregnant—like right now—tonight."

"I know that."

"What do you think about that?"

"I say let's do it."

My head snaps up. "What?"

"Let's go. I like you. You like me. I want to marry you. I told you that in so many ways. I want kids. You want kids. I think you would make an outstanding wife and mother. The only question is if you want to marry me and if you think I would make a good husband for you and father to our children. If you do, then what's stopping us? Let's go. I'm ready. I'm just over here waiting for you to be ready. If you aren't, then I want to know what it will take for you to be ready so I can do it and provide it and whatever else you need."

I blink at him trying to kick my brain back into gear. Why am I waiting? I'm medically clear and disease free. What do I need to be able to do this?

I don't see anything in Nate that would make me hesitate. He isn't the sticking point in my mind. I am.

I look away across the ocean. I had this idea in my mind that it might take me years to find the right person to do this with. What if I don't have to? What if he's sitting right here in front of me?

My mind switches gears—except that it doesn't. I've already been thinking this for ages. "All right. Let's do it."

Now his head snaps up. "What?"

"Let's do it. Let's go. I'm ready."

He blinks at me. "Are you serious? Like....right now?"

I laugh at him. "Yes, right now....unless you're on your period or something."

He flinches. Woops. He looks away. "I didn't think....I thought....you know....that you would have to warm up to it or something."

I lace my fingers into his. "So let's warm up to it. You're right. I'm ready and I want to do it. Let's start moving in that general directio n....."

"You mean like.....you would come up to my suite with me and spend the night?"

I can't help but burst into a beaming smile at him. "Yeah. That sounds nice."

He won't stop staring at me in shock. He really didn't expect me to say yes.

He finally stands up, squeezes my hand, and we head for the elevator. We're really going to do this.

Chapter 19: Holly

Nate and I stare at each other when we step inside the elevator. I don't know what I expected, but passion doesn't erupt right there in the elevator.

We both just stand there holding hands and looking at each other until the elevator opens on the top deck. We walk out and he heads for his suite.

It has exactly the same layout as mine with a living room and small kitchen in the center, a balcony overlooking the ocean, and two bedrooms off to each side.

This is definitely his suite. It smells like him. His laptop sits on the table with his new Bluetooth mouse and a few other electronics.

He leans against the back of the couch while I stand there at loose ends trying to figure out what to do next.

He doesn't say anything while I look around at everything—like his suite was somehow going to be so much different from mine.

"We don't have to do anything," he finally tells me. "We could just hang out and talk or watch a movie or anything like that. We don't have to jump straight into bed."

I try to deflect the tension by smirking at him. "You're the one who implied that I had to bed someone tonight to make some kind of statement about my freedom."

He chuckles. "Oh, yeah. I did imply that."

"So should I be dragging you off to my lair to have my way with you?"

His cheeks color and his eyes twinkle the way I know so well. "It looks like you're in my lair now."

"So what do you want to do to have your way with me?"

His eyes go hard again and his smile turns to a glare, but it's a glare of so much fiery passion that it almost scares me.

"Come here," he says.

I put my purse on the table and go over there. I don't know what he'll do, but I doubt he'll drag me off to his bed and take advantage of me. We aren't here for that.

I mean, we are here for that—just not in that way.

He slips his hand into mine, draws me between his knees, and wraps his arms around my waist.

He gives me one kiss and rears back to look down at me. "I'm really happy you're here," he tells me. "I know I say that all the time, but what I mean is that I'm really happy you're *here*. I'm glad we're going through with this. I'm glad it's finally happening and I'm glad I'm doing it with you. I can't think of any better way this could happen."

I blush at the way he's looking at me. "I feel the same way about you."

"Depending on how comfortable you are with all of this, we could make a rule that you have to initiate everything. Then we wouldn't do anything you aren't ready for...."

"No way!" I counter. "I'm not going to initiate everything!"

He frowns. "You aren't? I thought you would want to. I don't want to do something you don't want."

"I do want it. That's why I'm here. I don't want to be in charge of initiating everything. That isn't what I signed up for."

"So.....do you want me to initiate things?"

"Of course!" I exclaim. "Isn't that the man's role—to go all caveman and pursue and conquer and all that?"

He bursts out laughing. "Is that my role?"

"Sure. Didn't you know?"

He won't stop laughing. "I wasn't quite sure."

"I mean....I *could* initiate.....but I don't want to."

He fights his lips under control so he can look me in the eye. "So do you want me to initiate.....and pursue and conquer and all that?"

"Of course. I mean.....I don't want you to get violent about it....but yeah.....I don't know what to do. Do you?"

His smile evaporates and his eyes drill me to the core. "Yeah. I know what to do."

He eases in and kisses me. He starts lightly and doesn't try too hard to escalate.

He rocks me in his arms the way he usually does when we kiss. I wrap my arms around his neck and sink into the warmth of his lips, run my fingers through his hair, rub the back of his neck, and just enjoy being with him.

None of this is anything we haven't already done a million times before. I melt into him and my mind goes soft on the waves of satin bliss in his lips and tongue.

He tightens his arms around my waist and runs his hand up my back to my neck, but he doesn't escalate—at least, I don't notice it at first.

I don't know the moment when it happens. We kiss the way we always do, but it changes somewhere in the middle. It changes to something else.

We usually just kiss in a sensual, easy way because we both know it isn't going to go anywhere.

Somehow or other, the simple fact that this is going to go somewhere changes everything. We kiss in the usual way, but somewhere along the way, we get to a point where we both know we don't have to hold back anymore.

Our kisses change. They kiss deeper and the heat changes from something less passionately romantic to pure volcanic lava.

I gasp into his mouth as a wave of unbridled sexual fire torches through me. We're going all the way—right now—tonight—right here on the edge of the couch.

I don't feel his kiss as a soft, sensual, river of comfortable bliss. His kiss ignites my body in unimaginable ways.

I feel him kissing, licking, sucking, and teasing all over my body. He isn't kissing my mouth—not only my mouth.

He's between my legs. He's nibbling my breasts. His hands and mouth explore my whole body even though we're still only just kissing.

Our lips break apart in a ragged, panting gasp of short, agonized hunger. His eyes smolder with intense fury. Nothing will hold him back tonight.

He rears away just enough for him to glare down into my eyes. His lips shiver back from his teeth and his nostrils flare.

He grabs one of my breasts through my dress and squeezes while he snarls down into my face. A jet of fire rushes between my legs and my vision blurs when he crushes my breast in his hand and his fingers trail down it just enough to pinch my nipple.

He drags me closer to him until he crushes me in one muscular arm. His breath rasps through his bared teeth. He looks primal and furious and ravenous like this.

He lets go of me just as fast and grabs a big handful of my ass. My dress bunches in his hand and he takes the hint by pulling it up and diving his hand underneath it.

He holds my eyes with no mercy while he squeezes my ass again and works his hand deeper into the cleft where it meets the back of my thigh.

He comes within a fraction of an inch of feeling how wet he's making me. He uses that hold to pull me upward, but I can't get to him with my dress in the way.

Lightning quick, he scoops me up in his arms and pulls me onto his lap. He pries my thighs apart to straddle him and I feel his hard spike drilling into me from below.

I gasp and then moan when he sits me down on it. His hands go wild covering every part of my body.

He pulls down the short sleeves of my dress and then rips my bra aside so he can attack my chest. He arches his prick into me from below until I can't stop whimpering in an agony of desire.

I stifle a scream when his mouth closes on my breasts. He sucks hard and the rest of him gives me no rest, either.

He grabs my ass in both hands and pulls me into a steady thrusting rhythm even though our clothes still stop us from getting to each other.

I try to keep up with him, but I can't even get to his jacket when he comes at me this hard. I wind up just clasping his shoulders through his suit.

He doesn't have the same problem. He mauls my chest, gobbles up to my neck, and makes me yelp again when he nips my ears and shoulders.

He slides my dress all the way up and only pulls away long enough to lift it completely over my head and off.

He unclips my bra at the same time. Now I'm straddling him in my panties and nothing else.

He slows way down when he sees me naked. He eases off and leans back so he can look at me and watch his own hands traveling up, down, and everywhere.

He slides them up my thighs, circles my waist, cradles my breasts, strokes down my back and up to the back of my neck, and cups my cheeks to kiss me.

This position triggers an equally primal reaction in me. It turns me on more than I ever thought possible, but I have to hold onto him to stop myself from falling off.

Balancing on his lap throws all my weight down on his rock-solid package lying buried between my thighs.

I don't know how to take this any further, so I lean in, wrap my arms around his neck again, and kiss him.

He glides both arms around my waist and pulls me farther toward him.

He must have leaned too far because he loses his balance and topples backward onto the couch behind him. He yells out in surprise and I scream.

He definitely didn't do it on purpose because he rolls too far and almost pitches both of us onto the floor before he corrects.

He barely pulls me back in time and we wind up in a twisted, jumbled pile on the couch.

We both yell and groan when our weight falls against each other. He winds up landing on top of me. "Nate!!" I yell.

"Sorry!" he yells back. "That wasn't supposed to happen!"

We both wind up laughing. Pulling our twisted limbs out from under each other turns into a comical game of painful twister. We grunt and groan before we both collapse out of breath on the couch.

Chapter 20:
Holly

I flop in breathless exhaustion on the couch next to Nate. He's still wearing his suit. I'm not wearing anything but my panties, but the moment seems to have passed when we were going to do it.

Me lying here all but naked doesn't seem to mean anything anymore. He's just Nate and I'm just me the way we always have been. Nothing suddenly changed because he took my clothes off.

He throws his arm over the arm of the couch behind his head, wraps his other arm around my shoulders, and pulls me against him. "Maybe it's a sign from God that we aren't supposed to do it."

I laugh at him. "Leave God out of this, buddy. God has nothing to do with this."

He chuckles. "It's probably just as well. I might start to get jealous if he did."

I laugh some more and settle down next to him on the couch. It feels good to just cuddle up with him with no expectations or pressure that we might do something more.

He glances over at me with his cheeks glowing. "How about Alexis trying to hook up with more guys while she's still contagious, huh?"

He bursts out laughing. "I will never forget her getting busted by Troy in front of everyone! I really wish I could have gotten that on video."

I beam at him. "She definitely got what was coming to her. She doesn't know when to quit."

He looks over at me. "I feel so much better, now that I can laugh at her misfortune. She and Carlos aren't laughing at us anymore."

"They're both toads. I'm sure nothing will end well for either of them considering the way things are going."

"I'm sure Alexis will find some other chump to hook up with as soon as she gets the all-clear."

I raise my head to stare at him. "You are not a chump, Nate! You can't tell yourself that! You're a great guy. She didn't know how lucky she was until she lost you."

He won't stop gazing at me. "Yeah. You're right."

We wind up staring at each other—and that moment brings the passion flaring back to life. We both attack each other kissing as fast and hard as we possibly can.

I scramble to get on top of him and kiss him and straddle him the way I was before. I want him bad and I want him now.

He tries to pull his jacket off, but he can't when he's lying flat on his back.

He kisses me back just as hard and keeps getting distracted by my breasts and the rest of my body.

He finally grabs me around the waist, rears off the couch, and flips me onto my back before he dives down on top of me to maul my mouth.

He has just as much trouble getting his jacket and shirt off in this position as before. He lies all the way down on top of me and drives his hips between my legs to push my thighs apart.

I whimper and then moan into his mouth when I feel how hard he is. He throbs and swells every time he thrusts in.

He screws his hips in brutal little circles each time he does that and lets out a tiny little grunt of pure animal madness. His whole body strains with muscle trying to get inside as fast and hard as he can.

I claw at his jacket trying to kiss him fast enough and pull his clothes off at the same time. He finally gives up, rears onto his knees, tears his jacket and tie off, and unbuttons his shirt.

I don't want to wait. I sit up and start pulling his belt free while he's still working on his buttons.

I get his pants unzipped before he accomplishes that. I dive under his shirt, kiss and tease his stomach, and crawl down to the bulge in his shorts.

He reacts too fast, pushes me away hard enough to make me topple backward onto the couch, and I scream in surprise before he plunges between my legs to devour me.

He barely pulls my panties aside before he starts burrowing his way all the way into my swollen flesh. I yelp and then don't stop whining and sobbing in ecstasy as he increases the intensity.

He's too busy pulling the rest of his clothes and my panties off to do anything else, but all of that comes to an end as soon as he finishes undressing himself.

He seizes my thighs, pulls them farther apart, and lifts them higher to expose my raw, sensitive tissues for his enjoyment.

He nags me to screaming ecstasy in no time—and then gets his hands involved. He forks his fingers on either side of my clitoris to spread my petals and stretch them taut to make me howl in dizzy rapture.

He flickers his tongue over the most delicate parts of my flesh until I reel in the stratosphere, but he doesn't stop there.

He drives his fingers in until I can't take it anymore. I teeter into a blistering climax that doesn't end. He keeps plowing me full of his fingers, breaking me open, and wringing every last drop of passionate fulfilment from my soul.

I grab his head and hands, but I can't stop this. It's too big and satisfies something I didn't even know was missing. He gives me something I never got from Carlos. I'm not sure Carlos even knew it existed to give to me.

I'm still spiraling off into outer space when Nate scoops me up off the couch, sits down naked on the cushions, and pulls my legs around him the way we were before.

We aren't in any danger of falling over this time. He locks his eyes on my delirious face and eases me down on his shaft.

It glides in on a slippery, delicious path of juicy goodness. I droop in pure rapture when his thick meat fills me to the breaking point, but he won't just let me sit there and feel this overpowering sensation of completion.

He caresses my cheeks, follows my curves down my chest to my waist, and takes hold of my hips to guide me into his rhythm.

The intensity and power of this moment overtakes me and spins me off into another drunken trance of orgasmic cataclysm, but he doesn't let me stop.

He circles one arm behind my back and uses it to drive me down on him harder and faster.

The fingers of his other hand thread into my hair and he tightens his grip on my head to hold me there.

His eyes command me to find him. "Look at me," he husks. "Look and see....."

I cry out again when I see all the tortured emotion in his eyes. His beautiful heart radiates out of those eyes. I can hardly stand all the love pouring into me from him right now.

"You're mine, baby," he whispers. "Look at me and see. You're mine. You'll always be mine from now on no matter what. That's right. Give yourself to me. Give me your heart. That's right. You know you're mine. That's right. That's what you want, isn't it?"

I want it. I want it all. I want his body filling me with unstoppable pleasure right now, but I also want his heart. I want all that care and acceptance pouring into me from his eyes. I can't stand to lose any part of him, especially not that.

I'm so far gone in the stratosphere of passionate bliss that I can't even think. He slams me down on his shaft against and again. I can't stop and I don't want to.

He doesn't let me control the rhythm or the depths of those thrusts. He lifts me with his arm and brings me down at his own rhythm until I fly off in a whirlwind of out-of-control rapture.

His breathing quickens. His nostrils flare again and again as his body strains, but he doesn't stop until I explode in a screaming, crying convulsion of so many orgasms all on top of each other.

I collapse on his chest sobbing and whimpering as the last spasms ripple through my body. My brain shatters in all these explosive feelings rushing through me.

He doesn't let me rest. He picks me up, turns me around, kneels on the floor, and sits me on the couch.

He takes hold of my thighs, pulls them apart, and then draws me in so he can enter me again.

I collapse back on the cushions, but the couch holds me upright enough to see him driving into me from directly in front of me.

His hands clasp behind my ass to pull me into his thrusts, but his eyes keep overflowing with all those feelings that don't ever stop. This means as much to him as it does to me.

I get so consumed with how powerful and impossibly hot he looks that I can't even climax anymore. I stare up at him in the full majesty of his strength and love.

His eyes never release me. He wants to see me looking back at him with the same expression of unwavering love and decision that we're really doing this.

Right then, he moves one hand to my stomach. I don't know what he's going to do next. He takes me completely by surprise when he slides his thumb down to my clitoris and starts stroking me while he keeps drilling into me from below.

That extra little bit of sensation blasts me to smithereens. I can't stop screaming as I skyrocket away into another catastrophic series of orgasms.

He's getting me pregnant. That's what this is. Every thrust of his shaft into me plants his seed that will grow into our future.

Thinking that makes all of this so much hotter. I respond to him in ways I've never responded to anyone, not even Carlos.

My body wants to grow and ripen and produce for Nate. Thinking about getting pregnant and having a child with him excites me to the point of orgasm. I feel like I'm going to orgasm just from thinking about it.

He doesn't give me the option to think about it. He keeps giving me these insane climaxes again and again without stopping.

I barely finish that one before he climbs onto the couch. He plants his knees between my thighs and plunges into me from that position a few times, but I can't look up at him when I'm lying with my back hunched against the cushions.

He swivels me sideways, wraps my legs around his waist, and lies down all the way on top of me. He starts kissing me, but he doesn't look away. He keeps his head straight and his eyes open to lock on my very soul.

He holds eye contact no matter what as his body builds to an epic release. This is the moment. It's happening. He's about to get me pregnant.

We both see it in each other's eyes. There's no more room for doubt.

I hold that gaze no matter what. We're doing this one way or the other. It might not happen tonight, but it will happen if we keep doing it like this.

That moment gives both of us the clarity we need to check in with ourselves and each other—just to make sure we're really going through with this.

All doubt evaporates from my mind. I want this and I want it with him. Everything about this feels right.

I see the same truth written in his eyes. I only hope he sees it written in my eyes. We've come too far to fail now.

He gasps in my mouth once—and then again. His breath comes out in short, rapid bursts and then he grimaces as he floods me with his essence. His lips stop functioning for a second as the dam breaks and he unloads.

He clamps his eyes shut only for a second before they snap wide open to stare into the very depths of my being. I've never done it with anyone like this before. He's so incredibly beautiful and pure. I absolutely love that about him.

He doesn't stop staring at me even after it's over. He keeps gazing into my eyes and reading all the possibilities written there.

This is hands down the most meaningful sex I've ever had. I don't want to let him go. I want to wrap my arms around him and hold him near me forever.

He stays inside me while his body keeps twitching, swelling, and flexing to drain the last precious drops of him into me.

His strained breathing and the tension in his muscles turns me on even more than I was before. I could do it with him again right now, but he eases off and pulls out.

He doesn't go away or roll aside. He stays there between my legs staring at me and kissing me for the ages.

I don't want him to stop. I don't want the moment to come when we have to face reality or pay attention to anything other than each other.

I keep seeing so many future possibilities in his eyes and face. He never looks away. Untold emotion surges in his eyes. The muscles around them keep changing with all the hidden shades of possibility.

I don't look away or hide from those possibilities. Everything will be okay between us as long as we can always look each other in the eyes and see each other this way.

We both want the same things. We both want to work toward the same future.

I swim in the sea of all that he is. The vast depths of his personality open for me to explore everything about him.

He doesn't give me any warning before he rears off the couch taking me with him. He keeps his arms around me and my legs spread around his waist when he stands up and carries me into the bedroom.

I cling to him, but he holds me easily on our way across the suite.

He uses one hand to pull down the covers. He sits down on the edge of the bed, but he doesn't get into it.

He tightens his arms around me there, kisses me a few more times, and then buries his head and face in my neck in a deep, powerful, soul-aching hug.

He holds me so much tighter, now that we both finally know. We found each other. We're together at last.

I shut my eyes, rest my dizzy head on his shoulder, and clasp the back of his head. His hair falls in my eye and his sweat seeps into my skin all over my body.

I hug him back with all the love and powerful contentment overflowing from my soul. He's right. We're right. This is all right.

Holding him like this feels unimaginably good. I've never felt anything so good because we're together and it's right. Nothing can break us apart as long as we feel this way about each other.

Neither of us tries to sit up or kiss or turn it sexual. This means more—just being together like this.

We're together in more ways than just physically. We aren't just together in this room and on this cruise. We're together in our hearts and in our whole lives.

We'll build one life for both of us now.

Chapter 21: Nate

I float in the clouds somewhere above my bed and feel the luscious sensation of Holly's naked body on top of me.

She breathes evenly in semi-sleep, nuzzles into my neck, and her breasts, stomach, thighs, and hips caress every inch of me when she squirms. She's just waking up—or partially waking up.

I'm only partially awake, too. Daylight streams through the gauzy curtains in front of my balcony. The sea breeze makes them billow into the room.

They let cooling puffs of air into the room and stop it from getting too hot and stuffy.

I'm exhausted after enjoying Holly's delights all night long. I could take her again right now if I wasn't still half-asleep.

She is by far the most passionate woman I have ever been with. She's a hundred times more passionate than Alexis. I didn't think that was possible, but Holly is proving me wrong.

She connects with me at a deeper level while she does it. She doesn't just make sex hotter and more explosively fulfilling. She sees me and expresses a deeper bond than I ever knew was possible.

Maybe that deeper bond of connection is what makes the sex hotter. How do I know? I only know I can't get enough of her—but we both do need to sleep sometimes.

Just feeling her here in bed with me is somehow so much sweeter than taking her body all night long. Laughing with her on the couch after I fell over feels so much sweeter than sex could ever be.

I share that with her because it's her. I didn't know it was possible because no other woman is her. I could only have this with her. I couldn't experience it because I hadn't met her yet.

She squirms again, rolls off me, and pries herself out of bed to go to the bathroom. She washes her hands, staggers back to bed, and topples with her face buried in the pillow. "I'm dead," she mumbles. "Call the mortuary."

I laugh and kiss the side of her head before I collapse onto my back. Life is too good to move. "You smell too good to be dead. I'll call the mortuary when flies start buzzing around your rotting corpse."

She snickers and turns on her side so I can see her magnificent body stretched out all naked. I love seeing her like this—all soft and unguarded.

All her walls came down last night. They don't come back up when she smiles at me. It's a smile of open, relaxed, happiness just to be here with me. She's as happy about it as I am.

"Do you have anything you have to do today?" she asks. "Do you have to get up and function at any point? What about calling your family? Do you need to check in on your mom?"

"I don't have anything I absolutely have to do. I could call them later, but I don't have to." I lean over and kiss her on the temple again before I lie down. "One of my brothers will call me if anything happens. The last I heard she was cleaning out the fridge and the kitchen cabinets, so I take that to mean she's feeling better."

She laughs and runs her fingers through her hair. "I'd say so."

"What about you? What's on the program for you today?"

She smirks and kisses me. "Besides you? I don't have a program other than that."

"Don't try to flatter me. Do you need to do anything to take care of the divorce or are you going to wait until you get home to do everything?"

Her smile slips. "We should probably talk about that."

"Talk about what?"

"About what we're going to do when this cruise ends. You live in Seattle and I live in Spokane."

"So?" I ask.

"So....you have to go to Seattle to deal with your divorce with Alexis. I have to go to Spokane to deal with my divorce with Carlos. We won't see each other then and any number of things could happen while we're apart."

I look up at the ceiling. "You're right. We have some giants to slay before we ride off into the sunset. Or rather, I have to slay a few giants before I can rescue the fair maiden and ride off into the sunset."

She doesn't take the joke. She pushes herself up on her elbow. "Seriously. What are we going to do when this cruise ends? We need a plan if we're going to really do this."

I turn to face her. She looks so beautiful gazing down at me with her hair all messy. "Answer me this," I tell her. "Do you have family or anything in Spokane that would make you want to stay there? You must like your job a lot."

"I like my job, but I work remotely. I can work from anywhere."

I raise my eyebrows. "Don't you work for an agency or something—or a firm or something like that?"

"I work for an online agency. Everything is electronic, so I'm not tied down for work. All my family is in Seattle. The only thing I have left in Spokane is the divorce."

"Then how do you feel about moving to Seattle to live with me?"

She shrugs. "I feel fine about it. It sounds like a good plan."

"Then I'll take extra time off work to come back to Spokane with you until you finish off the divorce."

Her jaw drops. "You will? How would you do that?"

"I have a bunch of vacation and sick leave accrued with my job. I was saving it up to spend with Alexis and our future children, but I don't need to do it now."

"Really?!" she exclaims. "You would really come back to Spokane with me?!"

"Of course. I don't want to let you out of my sight—especially not with a dirtbag like Carlos around. You'll need support to get through the divorce. We should stick together. We can be together in Spokane and then you can come back to Seattle with me."

She bursts out in excited laughter. "Great! I can't wait!"

I smile at her. How happy she is makes me so mind-blowingly happy. She really wants to do this with me. It's all coming true.

She jumps up. "I want to get started now!"

"How would you do that?" I ask from the bed. "What all do you need to do to file the paperwork and everything?"

"I'm not sure. Have you looked into it?"

"Yes, I'm having my lawyer file it for me, but there's a waiting period. You have to have been living apart from the person for a certain number of months before you can file and then remarry."

She grimaces. "Ick. I hate all of that."

"What about selling your house and dividing the money?"

"That should be pretty straightforward. That will be the first thing I should do when I get back. In fact, I could be doing that now." She sits up and looks around. "Oh, damn. All my stuff is in the other suite."

"You can bring it here later." I grab her arm and pull her back into bed. "But not now. You're trapped in my lair and you can't get away."

"Can I be trapped in your lair and not get away while I eat breakfast?"

I laugh. "Only if you order enough for me."

She goes into the living room, comes back with the menu, and uses my phone to place the order.

We lounge in bed until the food comes. Then she puts on one of the fluffy bathrobes from the bathroom, meets the room service guy and tips him, and wheels the cart into the bedroom. "Don't get crumbs in the sheets," she tells me.

"Where's the fun in getting room service if we can't get crumbs in the sheets?" I ask.

"You're going to have to do all the housework with an attitude like that."

"I don't do housework. I have a housekeeper do it for me."

She looks up. "You do? Didn't Alexis do any cleaning?"

"Very little and that was more like entertaining. The housekeeper does the actually real cleaning."

She shakes her head and starts passing the food to me. "Wow. That's incredible."

"Why is it incredible? We aren't the only ones who use a housekeeper."

"I've never had one. No one in my family has ever had one. It isn't a thing in my family."

"What do you do instead?"

She laughs at me. "We clean, silly. We keep our houses clean. My mother, grandmother, and aunts would die of shame if they thought about someone else cleaning their houses or doing their laundry or doing their cooking or anything like that—on both sides—my mother's side and my father's side. We just don't do housekeepers. The wife and mother of the family is the housekeeper. In my family, that's what being a wife and mother means. It means keeping the house. They would feel like they weren't doing their job if they let another person do any of that."

"Wow," I remark. "That is so different from the way Alexis sees it."

"What about your mom? She's cleaning her own fridge and kitchen cabinets. She must do it that way, too."

"You're right. I never thought about it that way before. It just seemed like the thing to do when I married Alexis."

"How did she convince you to do it?"

"I can't remember how it came up. I don't know why. I just thought, 'Okay, whatever.'"

She shakes her head. "That would never happen with us, especially if we had kids."

"How do you mean? Doesn't it make more sense to have someone doing all those menial tasks to take the pressure off the mother?"

"No way!" she exclaims. "All those menial tasks are acts of love. Folding your kids' clothes after they come out of the laundry—cooking your kids' meals and packing their lunch boxes for school every morning—giving them baths and changing their sheets when they barf in the middle of the night......"

I can't help but laugh. "Fun times."

"Seriously. That's what being a mother means. It's what being a parent means. I don't see why you would want to outsource those jobs to someone else—so your kid can think of someone else that way instead of you? I would never let that happen."

I beam up at her. "You're really passionate about this, aren't you?"

"Well, that's the way I was raised. My mom did all of that for us—and so did my dad. That's what I love about them. They took the job seriously and they put their hearts and souls into it. The effort and sacrifice was an act of love and it showed. I would never want parents who did it any other way."

"You're right. My parents were the same way." I beam at her. "I'm really happy I'm with you. I'm almost happy Alexis cheated on me so I could get together with you."

She splits in a grin. "I feel the same way. I'm not happy they cheated, but it does seem to be working out for the better, doesn't it?" She jumps up. "I'm going to go get my stuff out of my suite. We can slouch around and be slugs together after that. I want to list the house on the market now so it sells as soon as possible. I'll contact Carlos about it. The realtors can email us the paperwork to sign while you and I are still on the cruise. Then we won't have any unnecessary delays."

She hustles into the next room and starts gathering up her clothes.

"Aren't you going to finish eating first?" I call after her.

"I'll eat when I get back!" she yells through the door. "I can eat while I'm on the internet."

She races out of the room. I don't want to get up, but her energy and enthusiasms infects me. I go get my phone and crawl back into bed to check it.

I find a message from my senior manager saying he wants to talk to me about when I'm scheduled to restart work—which is in ten days. I'll have to take that conversation as an opportunity to get my leave extended.

I check out a bunch of other messages from work. It's all straightforward and nothing I don't already know about.

I also answer a few emails from my lawyer about the divorce. I text my brother Liam and ask him to send the footage of Alexis's infidelity to the lawyer, but not without copying it first.

Liam is more than happy to oblige and says he'll make a second copy for me just in case.

Holly works on her phone in the bed next to me while we eat. We comment back and forth to each other while we work.

"Do you want me to leave while you have your call with your boss?" she asks.

"You don't have to. I might go into the living room so I don't feel like I'm talking to him with a naked woman in my bed."

She laughs. "I'm not naked anymore. See?"

"It's the principle of the thing. I need to get my game face on and I can't do that when I'm lying in bed."

I get up, put on my pants and shirt, and go out to the living room when the time comes for the call. She stays in the bedroom propped against her pillows and keeps doing things on her phone.

The time comes and I get a call from him. His name is Phil Greeley. He's a sixty-year-old hard-ass with a heart of gold and a voice like Clint Eastwood.

"How's the cruise going?" he rasps.

"It's going good. Some personal stuff came up at home since I've been here. I was wondering if I could get some more vacation time tacked onto the other end. This might not work for you if you wanted to talk about when I'm scheduled to come back."

"Actually that's what I wanted to talk to you about. We just had a senior management meeting and we don't think you're doing your best work as a traveling sales rep."

My heart sinks. "Why not? You never said anything about this in any of my performance reviews. You always said you were happy with my performance."

"I'm not talking about your performance. We've all been delighted with your performance. We couldn't be happier."

"Then what's the problem?"

"We just think you can do better. I'm retiring in six months and the company wants to hire someone now so I can train them to replace me. The company wants to promote you to regional sales manager. You would be training and supervising all the other sales reps who are currently doing your job. You would work with me until I bring you up to speed and then take over for me when I leave."

I have to gulp to get my parched throat working. "You're....you're promoting me?"

"It's a local job in the Seattle office. You wouldn't have to travel anymore. You can go home to your family every night. What do you say?"

I swallow hard. "That would be great. I accept."

He laughs in his usual scratchy way. "Terrific. Now let's talk about how much leave you want to take. You can take as much as you want as long as it isn't more than....I'd say a month."

I glance toward the bedroom. "That won't be necessary. I don't need a month."

"Let's call it three weeks, then. Oh, by the way, the job has an annual salary. It isn't commission-based the way your sales job is. So I'll put the paperwork through now and you'll start drawing your salary now—while you're still on leave. Okay?"

I can barely choke out, "Um...okay. Thank you, Phil."

He laughs. "You earned it, son. Enjoy the rest of your vacation."

He hangs up and I sink back on the couch staring at my phone. Did that just happen? I got the job of my dreams—and right on time.

I have another three weeks of vacation time—more than enough to travel to Spokane with Holly and support her to finalize her affairs with Carlos.

I'm even getting paid to do all that. I'm drawing a paycheck right now while I'm on this cruise.

Holly comes out of the bedroom and sits next to me. How do I even begin to tell her about this? All my dreams are coming true. I don't know if I can handle it.

She doesn't ask. She just slips her hand into mine and squeezes. We're going to do this. She'll be there for me during all our triumphs and defeats.

This one played in my favor, but they won't all go that way. Some will go disastrously against us, but that's okay because we'll face them together.

Chapter 22: Holly

I glance out the window of the airplane as it taxies to the terminal in Spokane. I squint toward the terminal building and cover my eyes to groan.

"What's wrong?" Nate asks. "Are you going to puke?"

"I think I might have to. Carlos is in the terminal waiting for us."

Nate raises his eyebrows. "He sure didn't waste any time. Where is he?"

He bends over to look out the window. We can see Carlos standing in the boarding area behind the glass walls. He stares out at the plane as it parks and powers down its engines.

Nate sits back and starts getting his carry-on bag out from under the seat in front of him. "He must be really desperate."

"What should we do about him? He's probably here to cause a scene."

"Then let him. Airport security will deal with him. He'll probably get arrested again."

I make a face and look away, but I don't want to look out the window again. Carlos being here is really throwing a bucket of cold water on me coming home from the cruise with Nate.

"I suppose I should have expected something like this," I mutter.

"You were going to have to deal with him sooner or later. If he doesn't fall on bended knee and beg you to take him back here, he would do it at your house when you show up to move your stuff out. You wouldn't have TSA security guards there to do it for you."

I can't help but make another face. "I don't want to deal with him at all."

"It's only for a little while. You said he works here as a hospital administrator."

"Yeah. What about it?"

"Then he won't be able to follow you when you move back to Seattle. He'll have to stay here—if he even has a job anymore. I wonder if Troy told anyone about Carlos spreading gonorrhea to all those women. Some Good Samaritan might report it to the hospital. They might find out he was doing the same thing with countless women around the hospital. That wouldn't go so well for him."

I stare at the side of his face. "Are you saying you would do that—or that you did do it?"

"I'm not saying anything. I'm just saying someone might let it slip. It isn't the kind of behavior that speaks very highly of someone who's supposed to be running a public health facility, is it?"

I face front. I have to concentrate on getting off the plane.

I have to deal with Carlos all too soon. He hustles up to me the minute Nate and I get off the plane.

"Thank goodness you're back!" Carlos exclaims.

"What do you want?" I growl out the side of my mouth. "You shouldn't be here."

"We can work this out, Holly," he insists. "I still love you and I know you still love me."

"That's stretching it, pal."

"Come on! We have too much history to just throw our relationship away on a misunderstanding."

I push past him to keep walking. "Our history is the misunderstanding, Carlos. We're finished because I do understand now. I didn't before, but I do now. Now leave me alone. I never want to see you again."

He doesn't listen. He keeps following me down the concourse. "We would be fine now if *he* didn't come between us. You have to give me another chance."

I round on him spitting tacks. "He didn't come between us, Carlos! You did that! You were the one who destroyed our marriage—no one else."

Right then, a group of airport security guards pulls up. "Is everything all right here, folks?" a stout young man asks us.

"It's fine," Carlos tells him. "She's my wife."

"Ex-wife!" I snap and I turn to the guards. "I just told this man multiple times to leave me alone and that I didn't want to see him again. I'm going to get my luggage right now. I should not see your face again in this airport or at any other time, Carlos."

I turn on my heel and storm off. I'm too pissed even to look at Nate.

Carlos tries to follow us, but the guards get in his way and stop him from going anywhere.

We don't see him again before we get our luggage and our rental car. Nate drives to a temporary rental apartment we got just for two weeks while we're here in Spokane.

I flop on the bed. "Isn't there any way I can get through this divorce without seeing him again?"

"Do you want me to go over to your old house and pack up your stuff?" he asks. "Something tells me it would work better if you were there."

I snort. "Thanks. I'm really glad you're here."

He only smiles at me. We've both been saying that non-stop since we first met.

We spend the rest of the day doing some grocery shopping so we don't have to keep going out to restaurants to eat. We'll start cooking in our apartment and living as normal a life as we can for as long as this lasts.

I log into my laptop when we get back the apartment. I start getting organized to go back to work.

"Tomorrow is Monday," I tell Nate. "Carlos has to work. I'll go by the house while he's out and get the rest of my stuff. Then I don't have to go back at all."

"How much stuff do you have? Do we need a moving truck or anything?"

"No, I only have boxes—no big furniture or anything. I'll put everything in storage until we're ready to take it to Seattle, but we can do that anytime. We don't need to do that in the next two weeks. I just need to get everything out of the house as quickly as possible."

I go into the kitchen to take a casserole out of the oven. I'm cooking dinner for me and Nate tonight.

I'm in the middle of setting the table when I get an unstoppable wave of nausea. I have to rush into the bathroom before I puke into the toilet.

Nate follows me and leans against the counter until I finish. "What was that about?" he asks. "Did you get food poisoning on the cruise?"

"I don't know," I husk and rinse my mouth out in the sink. "I feel terrible."

I take a few steps toward the bedroom to lie down, but I lose my balance. Nate catches me and lowers me onto the bedspread. I start shivering in a cold sweat.

He rubs my back and goes to get his phone. "I think we better take you to the hospital. I don't like this."

I groan. "I don't need this right now."

He starts dialing on his phone and then puts it on speaker so I can hear. "Sacred Heart Hospital," a chipper woman's voice answers. "You're speaking with Judy. How can help you this evening?"

"Hi, Judy," Nate replies. "My girlfriend just started having violent nausea and vomiting for no reason. We just got home from a cruise and we think she might have gotten food poisoning. Do we need to go to the emergency room for that or should we go to the urgent care clinic?"

"How many episodes of vomiting has she had?"

"Just one. It just started a few minutes ago."

"Is there a chance your girlfriend could be pregnant?"

Nate spins around fast and his eyes pop when he stares at me. I stare back at him as the penny drops.

"Sir?" Judy asks. "Are you there?"

"Uh.....yeah.....I'm here......" he stammers. "Uh......let me call you back."

He hangs up. Neither of us can stop staring at each other. He barely speaks above a whisper. "Is this....is this real?"

I stagger off the bed, blunder into the living room, and get my phone out of my purse before I stumble back to bed.

My head reels all the way there. I can't stay upright. "It hasn't been two weeks since my last period," I tell him after I pull up my period log on my phone. "I shouldn't be showing any symptoms yet."

"Anything is possible, though, right?" he asks.

I switch to my calendar app and shake my head. "If this is right, it means I got pregnant that very first night. I don't see how it could be any other way."

He snorts and then explodes in laughter. He grabs me and tackles me sideways onto the bed. "Ha ha! It worked! You're pregnant! We're gonna have a baby! It worked!"

"Nate!" I scream and I have to fight my way out of his arms so I can run to the bathroom in time to hurl into the toilet again.

I collapse shaking onto the floor as the retching gets worse. I can't move.

He sits down next to me on the floor, rubs my back, and pulls my hair out of the way. "This is wonderful," he murmurs in my ear. "This is going to be the best thing that ever happened to us."

"Yeah, it's wonderful," I grumble. "You can take over for the rest of the night."

He snickers, but he doesn't laugh out loud.

I puke a few more times before he helps me back to bed. "Do you want to try to eat something?" he finally asks. "You know they say it's worse on an empty stomach. I'll bring it in here if you want some."

"I guess so," I mumble.

He leaves. I can barely get out of bed long enough to change into my pajamas.

He comes in with the casserole scooped into two bowls with spoons. That's dinner for tonight.

He props himself on the pillows next to me. I can't even sit up to eat. I raise my head just enough to spoon the food into my mouth before I collapse back. I have to stay flat no matter what.

"Let's make a doctor's appointment for tomorrow," he tells me. "We can confirm that it really is that and you can get a prescription for some kind of nausea suppressant."

"Fine," I tell him. "But we're still going to the house to get my stuff. I don't want to put it off any longer than necessary."

He makes the call to set up the doctor's appointment, but he can't get one until later in the afternoon anyway.

"That works out perfectly," I tell Nate after he hangs up. "I'm more interested in clearing my stuff out of the house and separating my life from Carlos than I am in getting pregnant."

"Aw, come on," he chides. "You know you want to find out if it's really that. I understand that you have to moan and groan because you feel terrible, but you're as happy about this as I am. Admit it."

"I'm happy about it, but I have nine whole months to confirm if I'm pregnant. I don't need to rush that. I don't really need to rush anything. I've been trying to get pregnant for so long, but now that I am, I can take my time. I have plenty of time to get ready before anything happens."

He looks up at me. "You sound awfully certain that you are pregnant."

I look away. "Call it a hunch."

Chapter 23: Nate

I keep casting glances through the windows of Holly's and Carlos's house while she packs up her things. I keep expecting him to come home in the middle of the workday to give her a hard time.

She goes through the house like a tornado—except that she doesn't make nearly as big a mess.

We bring flattened moving boxes, tape them together in the entrance hall, and she goes through the place systematically room by room.

She tosses stuff into the boxes as fast as she can go, stacks them by the door for me to tape shut, and keeps right on going.

I have to rush to keep up with her, take the boxes out to the car, and drive them to the storage unit before I come back for the next load.

She doesn't take the time to pack anything neatly or carefully. She doesn't fold any of her clothes when she gets to the bedroom. She pitches all her clothes, shoes, makeup, perfume, and purses into boxes and plows right on ahead.

We finish the whole job in a few hours. She takes a few family pictures of herself and her relatives off the shelf in the living room. She leaves behind every picture with Carlos in it.

She also leaves her engagement ring and wedding band on the hall table by the front door before she dusts off her hands and turns to me. "That's it. We can get out of here."

I lean and kiss her once. "Are you sure you don't want to do it here with me just once to stick it to him?"

She snorts and pushes me away. "We can do it anytime. We don't need to do it here."

I laugh. "Are you sure you don't want to get sex stains all over his bed?"

She bites back a smirk. "I might if I thought I could get away with that without seeing his reaction afterward. Let's go."

We drive the last load of boxes to the storage unit. She's still feeling weak even though she didn't act like it while she was moving out of that house.

Maybe she channeled her upset stomach into disgust for Carlos and motivation to move out of the house.

I take her out for lunch even though she isn't hungry. "You're going to have to eat sometime," I tell her. "You can't grow a baby on fumes."

"The doctor better give me something for all this nausea. I can't go nine months like this."

"They say it only lasts as long as the first trimester."

"Did any of your sisters-in-law have it?" she asks.

"No, they all sailed through without a peep. Oh, no, wait. I lied. My younger brother Todd—his wife had it real bad. I forgot about that. She didn't have to get hospitalized, but Todd and the doctors were talking about it there for a while. It did last the whole pregnancy, though. It didn't go away."

She makes a face and turns away. "I don't need to hear that."

I clasp her hand across the table while I stuff fries in my mouth with the other. "Come on, sweetheart. Don't resent me for being happy about this."

"I don't resent you for being happy about this—not at all. I'm happy about it, too, but who am I going to complain to if I don't complain to you? I have you as a captive audience."

I laugh again. Everything about this situation makes me happy, even the fact that she feels sick.

I drive her to the doctor's appointment after lunch. She wilts in the waiting room and rests her head on my shoulder until the nurse comes for us.

The doctor gives her a pregnancy test and it comes back positive. I shoot her a wild grin of pure excitement, but she only says, "I had a feeling it was that."

The doctor treats her morning sickness like it's the most insignificant thing in the world. He gives her a prescription and sends her on her way.

She reclines the car seat the minute she gets into the car, lies all the way down flat, and groans. "Make it end," she grumbles.

I squeeze her hand. "I'm about to. We'll go fill this prescription and then we'll go home and have dinner."

"Don't talk about food."

I have to stop myself from laughing. It's happening! I'm going to be a father. I can't wait.

I leave her in the car while I go into the pharmacy to fill the prescription. I also get a bottle of water before I take everything back to the car.

"Here you go," I tell her. "You can take it right now."

She sits up just long enough to down the pills. Then she lies down for the rest of the drive back to the apartment.

"I have to meet with my lawyer on Thursday," she tells me on the way inside. "Depending on what he says, we might be able to go back to Seattle earlier than we thought. I probably won't have to come back unless we have a hearing or a mediation or something."

"We still have some time in the apartment before I go back to work. We should take the time to move your stuff to my house. Then we won't have to come back here later."

We enter the building and ride the elevator to our floor.

"How are you feeling now?" I ask her in the elevator.

"I feel kinda normal. I think those drugs are really working."

"Great," I tell her. "Maybe this won't be as bad as we thought."

I squeeze her hand and she squeezes back. She smiles up at me—and we both know. We're going to be parents. She's pregnant and we're going home to my house in Seattle. Everything is working out the way we planned.

We get out of the elevator and the hair stands up on my arms when I see Carlos waiting for us outside the apartment. Tension and hostility spikes between me and Holly when Carlos turns around to face us.

"Holly made it pretty clear that she doesn't want to see you, man," I tell him. "I'm going to have to report you for harassment and stalking if you don't back off."

His dark eyes dart from me to her. "I know you got a pregnancy test and I know you got a prescription for morning sickness suppression."

She gasps and rolls her eyes to Heaven. "Did you use your influence at the hospital to find that out? Let me guess. You followed us to the appointment. You are such a creep, Carlos. Seriously. Get a real life."

She walks past him to get to the apartment, but he dodges in front of her. "I want a paternity test! This could be my child!"

"No, it couldn't!" She spins around and barely keeps her temper in check to snap at him instead of going completely postal right here in the hallway. "Don't you remember, you brainless sleazeball! You infected me with gonorrhea and gave me inflammation in my uterus that stopped me from getting pregnant! There is no way I could have gotten pregnant the whole time I was with you—thanks to you! This is not your child! Now leave me alone and don't come near me again! The next time I see your face, I'm calling the Police!"

He doesn't back off. He leans forward and gets right in her face. "I want a paternity test. If you don't get one, I'll take you to court and force you to get one. This will be a condition of the divorce. You will never get rid of me until I get it—and if this is my child, you can bet your ass I'm going to be in this child's life for the rest of eternity."

He storms off. He doesn't wait for the elevator. He blasts into the stairwell and takes off running down the stairs to leave the building.

He leaves Holly and me standing there with those words trembling in the air. She can't get a divorce until she gets a paternity test.

My mind tumbles in all kinds of weird directions. What if this baby isn't really mine? What if something went wrong and she really could have gotten pregnant before she got together with me?

I see the same doubts playing in her mind. She takes one look at me and walks into the apartment.

She doesn't stay in the living room. She goes into the bedroom and shuts the door.

I leave her there alone. I don't blame her for needing to take some time to herself. Carlos already ruined her life in more ways than one.

Now he's waiting until she starts to rebuild and gets some happiness for herself before he comes back to do it all over again.

I sit on the couch and stare out the window for a while. I can expect the same thing from Alexis. Those two are going to be a thorn in our sides for a long time.

She has every right to be upset that he's demanding a paternity test, but I'm actually happy about it. I better find out one way or the other right now.

I already know what the result will be. She hasn't been out of my sight since we got together. She couldn't have gotten with anyone else and she couldn't have gotten pregnant before we got together.

She acts way too loving toward me to be interested in someone else. She isn't that kind of woman. She's a one-man woman. She gives everything when she gives herself to anyone at all.

I already know that about her, but his demand still raises all those doubts in my mind. I have to know. She has to know. He has to know. So this test will be a good thing.

She comes out of the bedroom after an hour and flops on the couch next to me. "Sorry," she mumbles. "I shouldn't have shut you out like that."

"It's okay. You don't have to apologize to me for needing your space. You needed to deal with this in your own way. There's nothing wrong with that."

She looks up at me and tears brim in her eyes. "It's your baby, Nate. I need you to know that."

"I do know it, sweetheart. You don't have to worry about me."

"I mean....." She passes her hand across her forehead. "What if something went wrong? What if Dr. McKinlay made a mistake and I really could have been fertile before I got with you? What if....what if I'm saddled with Carlos for the rest of my life and we have to co-parent a child together?"

"Hey! Baby!" I grab her hand, and when that doesn't work, I cup her cheeks to turn her toward me. "Look at me! Listen to me! Do you remember what you told me? You didn't start your fertile days until after you came on the ship. Carlos and Alexis did it with each other and all the infidelity stuff came to light before you became fertile. Remember?"

She nods fast with tears streaking down her cheeks.

"You couldn't have gotten pregnant before that even without the gonorrhea and you never slept with him after you found out about the infidelity. He's not the father. I am. You have nothing to worry about."

She fights her lips too hard to answer. She looks so miserable. I love that she's suffering from the same doubts. She wants more than anything for me to be the father.

I pull her into my arms and she breaks down sobbing on my chest. Poor thing. I could snap Carlos in half for hurting her like this.

The truth is that I'm too grateful even to care about him. I don't hate him. I just think he's a dope for not realizing what a good thing he had when he was with her.

He fouled his own nest and now he can't live with it. He's too stupid even to own up to how badly he screwed his own life.

Now she's mine. That's his loss.

What's the worst that could possibly happen? If this is his child—which it isn't—Holly and I would just raise the child as our own.

This child would grow up alongside our own children. Our oldest would occasionally go to stay with their biological father. Lots of families have to do it that way. It's no big deal.

I don't tell her that because I don't want to introduce even more doubt into her head. She's already struggling enough as it is.

Chapter 24: Holly

I curl my lip at the office building in front of me. "That snake is in there."

"The paternity results are in there," Nate tells me. "This is the last time you ever have to see Carlos. We'll meet with him, our lawyer, his lawyer. Your house is sold. You two will split the money, we'll get the paternity results, and we'll drive straight home to Seattle. Your nightmare will be over."

"It better be," I mutter.

He squeezes my hand. "Come on. Let's get it over with. Then we can put it all behind us."

He gets out of the car, opens my door for me, and helps me out. We hold hands on our way into the building.

I could puke again just from the thought of seeing Carlos. The anti-nausea medication is taking care of my morning sickness, but the thought of being in the same room with him brings it all back with a vengeance.

It's a good thing there will be three other grown men in the room to stop me from tearing the little twerp's eyeballs out.

I really hope Carlos's lawyer knows the whole story behind our breakup. I hope the guy realizes what a sleaze Carlos really is.

Nate doesn't give me a chance to question or hesitate. We find out from the receptionist where we're supposed to go, ride the elevator to the tenth floor, and walk down a carpeted hallway to the conference room.

Carlos and his attorney stand on the other side of the table. My attorney sits on this side. His name is Pete Hargraves. He's a young guy with glasses and a bookish manner.

He doesn't seem hard enough or brutal enough to handle himself in a courtroom or highly charged legal setting, but he sure knows his stuff.

Carlos's lawyer is a thick-set, burly, Latino guy named Pedro Alvarez. He has a small, neatly trimmed black goatee and curly black hair.

He really does look hard enough and brutal enough to handle himself pretty much anywhere, including in a dark alley with some much larger assailants. He looks like he could eat Pete for lunch.

I shake hands with Pete and all five of us approach the table. Pete, Nate, and I stay on this side. Pedro and Carlos stay over there like we're about to engage in the Battle of Little Bighorn.

"We're here to settle the matter of *Holly Patton Silverman vs. Carlos Silverman,*" Pete begins. "This meeting will serve as binding arbitration of their divorce settlement. Any agreements reached in this meeting will be binding on all parties. The parties agree only to seek jurisdictional remedy in the event that arbitration fails. Do we all agree?"

Carlos and I both nod.

"Let's begin with the matter of paternity of Ms. Silverman's unborn child," Pete goes on. "Mr. Alvarez and I have both received sealed copies of the results. No one has seen the results before now. He and I will both unseal our results at the same time. These results will be considered binding on all parties unless some discrepancy in the results suggests an error with the testing process. Is that agreed?"

Carlos and I agree. Pete and Pedro both take out sealed manila envelopes and tear them open at exactly the same time.

They check the results, hand each other their papers, and then hand the results to me and Carlos.

"The test results indicate that Mr. Silverman is not the father of Ms. Silverman's child and that Mr. Whitman *is* the father," Pete goes on. "Mr. Silverman's paternity claim is therefore denied and all rights denied."

Nate grabs my hand and bursts into a huge grin. He barely stops himself from laughing right there.

Carlos throws the paper on the table and curses under his breath. Pete and Pedro both pretend not to notice. What a chump.

"We now turn to the matter of dissolution of property," Pete goes on. "The parties agree that the house at 268 Mortons Road will be sold and the proceeds divided equally between Mr. Silverman and Ms. Silverman. The property has been sold and the proceeds transferred to escrow. The escrow officer will transfer funds to Mr. and Ms. Silverman's bank accounts." He looks up at Pedro and Carlos. "Do you gentlemen have any other matters to raise?"

"Yeah, I do," Carlos interjects. "I want to know about the....."

Pedro stops him by raising his hand. He actually straightens his arm and presses the edge of his hand against Carlos's chest.

Carlos spins around. Pedro gives him a look of ice-cold command before Pedro turns back to Pete and me. "We don't have any other matters to raise," Pedro goes on. "That's all we need to take care of. The parties agree. We can put this matter to rest. The funds from the sale of the house should go out within the next week." He holds out his hand to Pete and then to me. "It was a pleasure meeting with you."

Pete, Nate, and I stand up. We shake hands with Pedro and then he gives Carlos another death glare to make him shake hands with us, too.

Pete walks out with us. We don't hear Pedro and Carlos talking in the conference room until the three of us get far enough away not to understand their conversation.

"That went well," Pete remarks once we get into the elevator.

"Thank you so much, Pete," I breathe. "You were great."

He smiles at me. "We don't usually get guys like him on the other side. You dodged a bullet with that one."

I laugh nervously. Nate won't stop grinning and blushing like a crazy man.

"Do you know Pedro very well?" I ask in the building lobby.

"Oh, sure," Pete replies. "He's a great guy. He knows how to handle his clients."

"He seems like it," I murmur.

He smiles at both of us and shakes our hands. "I wish you all the best. Contact me if you need anything else or if you have any trouble with the transfer of funds from escrow. You should be all clear after that goes through."

Nate holds it together just long enough for us to get back in the car. Then he explodes in wild laughter, seizes me, and hugs me. "Whoo-hoo! The test was positive!" He yells out the window. "This baby is mine!"

A few people passing on the street give him weird looks. I stifle laughter. "Quiet down before you get arrested."

He won't stop laughing when he finally rolls up the window. "Suck on it, you cheating scumbag! Take it all the way to the bank. Now we can go back to Seattle where we belong."

He drives us to our rental apartment and we both get busy packing up all our belongings. It doesn't take long because we both knew we would leave here soon.

We've also spent the last few days trucking all my worldly possessions to his house in Seattle. We have no more reason to stay in Spokane.

I fold all my clothes into my suitcase except for the outfit I plan to wear tomorrow for the drive across the state.

I wheel my suitcase into the living room and get out the leftovers from yesterday's dinner. I don't want to make extra when I can just use up what we already have.

I put the dish in the microwave while I put all our extra groceries and a few kitchen items in shopping bags. Nate comes out of the bedroom with his suitcase. "Let's leave tonight," he tells me.

My head snaps up. "What?"

"Let's leave tonight. I don't want to stay. We'll drive all night and get there in the morning. What do you say? Why wait? We can sleep in our own house tomorrow and start settling in."

I blink at him and then shrug. "Okay. Let's just eat some dinner first. Then we can hit the road."

He laughs again and scoops his arms around my waist. "We're going to have a wonderful life."

He kisses me and then hustles outside to go put everything in the car. We've already traded our rental for his car that we picked up on one of our runs to Seattle.

I heat up the food, set out plates at the table, and then go through the apartment cleaning everything. We won't be coming back here again ever.

I take extra time to clean the kitchen and bathrooms. Nate comes in and we sit down to eat, but neither of us lingers over the food. We feed ourselves and then both get to work clearing all our possessions out of the apartment.

I run the dirty dishes through the dishwasher, put everything away, and wipe down the counters. The place looks as good as it can.

Nate gives me one more grin of mischievous knowing before we walk out the door. He drops off our keys at the manager's office and we get into the car.

"So long, Spokane!" he crows when he starts the motor. "It's been fun, but it's time to go."

"Don't cry too much when we're gone," I add. "You still have Carlos to keep you company."

Nate laughs and puts the car in gear. We settle in for the long drive back to Seattle for the last time.

Chapter 25: Holly

Nate pushes open the door to his house and holds it aside for me to enter. His house is huge compared to the house I shared with Carlos.

The entrance hall is a little mini-garden greenhouse with ceiling windows and a low sunken gravel bed with some tropical trees growing in there. It also has a water feature that constantly trickles and makes me feel like I'm in a forest or something.

A deck of smooth, polished cedar boards surrounds the bed. A few benches line the walls where a person can sit and just enough the atmosphere.

The hall leads to some steps that go down into the main living room. It's a big, sprawling, modern living room with pale beige carpet and beige and stone-grey furniture.

Sliding glass doors open from the living room onto another huge deck spread out in a big backyard. Tall cedar trees hide the yard from everything. It feels totally private and cut off from the world.

A giant stone fireplace covers one wall of the living room with a sleek, modern open-plan kitchen on one side of the living room.

Long hallways lead off the living room to large, semi-detached bedroom suites in different wings of the house.

Nate stands back while I walk around looking at everything. I can definitely see why he needs a housekeeper for a place like this. It's enormous and pristine. It would take a long time to keep it clean.

I can't really see kids living here, but maybe that's just because I never spent any of my childhood in a house like this.

The backyard is perfect for kids to go exploring. A high brick wall surrounds the yard with all those trees on the inside. My curiosity makes me want to go out there and see what's behind the walls and in all those stands of trees.

Nate comes up behind me. "What do you think? Do you like it?"

"It's stunning," I whisper.

"But do you like it? Do you think you could be comfortable here?"

"You're here. Of course I would be comfortable here."

"I want to make sure you're happy and you feel at home." He takes my hand. "Come over here. I want to show you something."

He leads me down one of the side halls. The hall opens into four different guest rooms before it turns off into a fully detached master bedroom suite.

Glass double doors open onto the master bedroom's own private deck. The deck overlooks a smaller but much more pristine Oriental garden manicured to the tiniest detail.

Two leather couches sit inside the glass doors so a person can enjoy the garden without actually going outside. That must be nice when the weather isn't good.

The bed is a giant king-sized sleigh bed with massive curved oaken head and foot boards.

The wall behind the bed open at both ends leading into a long his-and-hers walk-in closet with the master bathroom behind that.

Nate leads me to the bed, sits down on it, and pulls me toward him to wrap his arms around me. "This is going to be our room," he murmurs. "I want you to change anything you want and make it your own."

I fold his head in my arms and sway in the delicious relaxation of kissing him. We still haven't unpacked the car of all our stuff from Spokane after our all-night road trip to get back to Seattle.

We can do that later, though. Right now, Nate and I are toppling into bed. We both need sleep, but we need each other more.

All the obstacles are falling away. I'll be divorced soon and so will he. We'll get married and have our first child. Life will get busy when we both go back to work. Things will get complicated and messy.

I don't care about any of that. He's here and I'm here. I'm in his bed and his hands start to explore my body while we roll in each other's arms kissing.

He tumbles me onto my back, crawls between my legs, and I sigh in bliss while I feel his body tense as the strain builds.

I'm too tired to keep my eyes open. Softening into him feels half like going to sleep and half like flying. I don't need to see anything. I just need to float in this dream come true.

How magnificent the house and bedroom are—that doesn't mean anything as long as I'm with him. He's the same man from the cruise. He's the same man from our apartment in Spokane.

I loved him then when the accommodation wasn't nearly so luxurious. I love him as much now if not more.

My body responds to him instantly. I'm pregnant with his child. I'm going to give birth to all his children and mother them better than any mother in history.

Everything he does excites me and fulfills my deepest fantasies. I release myself into his hands and ride the waves of bliss into the stars.

He works off my mouth and burrows into my neck. He mauls down to my shirt collar and starts nuzzling into my chest.

The doorbell rings right then. It comes from the living room, but something amplifies the noise so we can hear it on the other side of the house.

Nate raises his head to listen and then groans and goes back to using his teeth to pull my shirt buttons undone.

I close my eyes only for the doorbell to ring a second time. He gasps in exasperation and climbs off me. "It better not be the Girl Scouts again."

I follow him out to the living room. I hang back behind the trees while he answers the door.

A young man with sandy brown hair and freckles stands outside. He smiles broadly when Nate shows up.

"Nate Whitman?" the guy asks.

"Yeah?" Nate asked. "What do you want?"

The guy holds out a large manila envelope. I'm really starting to hate those.

"You've been served," the guy replies. "Have a great day."

He walks off and leaves Nate standing there staring at the envelope. Served—for what?

He shuts the door and comes back inside still frowning at the envelope like it's a bomb about to go off.

"What are you being served for?" I ask.

"I have no idea. I'm not involved in any legal disputes. The divorce with Alexis is cut and dried."

"You better find out what it's for."

We retreat into the living room. All thought of getting close to each other goes right out of our heads.

He sits down on the couch and I sit next to him while he tears open the envelope. He pulls out a stack of papers and starts flipping through them one page at a time.

"Oh, my God!" he breathes.

"What?" I ask. "Are you being sued or something?"

"Alexis is pregnant. She's suing for paternity. She's demanding that I get tested to establish me as the father."

"But……" I think fast. "Could she have gotten pregnant on the cruise?"

"She could have, but she couldn't have gotten pregnant from me on the cruise because we never did it on the cruise. We were only on the cruise for one night before the whole infidelity thing blew up and we didn't do it that night. If she got pregnant on the cruise, it had to be from Carlos or someone else."

I frown at the papers. "Is he named in the suit?"

He goes back to flipping the pages. "The suit names him and another guy named Ed Conway." He snorts. "The filing lists him as her fiancé."

"That was quick. How can he be her fiancé when she's still legally married to you?"

"Exactly." He actually grins at me. "She's getting him tested, but there's no way he could be the father."

"How do you know?"

"Ed Conway is a technician at an IT outlet in town. I know the guy. He services computers for my company. Alexis and I took our devices there for repair a few times."

I place my hand on Nate's back. I would like to distract him from all of this and maybe get him to take me back to the master bedroom.

He doesn't even feel me touch him. He just keeps reading the paperwork.

I sigh. Now we have to deal with this. First it was mine. Now it's his.

I go into the kitchen and start hunting around to see what's in here that I can use to make breakfast.

I could start unpacking the car, but I don't want to leave Nate alone when he's so concerned about this.

"I don't suppose you know where Alexis was in her cycle when you went on the cruise, do you?" I call over. "We might be able to figure out when she got pregnant."

"She just finished her period a couple of days before we left. I remember because we were joking around about it and saying she better not still be on it when we went on the cruise. It ended right before we left and she joked around saying now she could do it as much as she wanted." He stands up and makes a face at me as he walks over to the kitchen counter. "I didn't know at the time she meant she could do it as much as she wanted with other guys. I thought she meant me. She obviously wanted me to understand it that way."

"Then there really is no way you could be the father. She wouldn't have been fertile in the few days between when her period ended and when you stopped having sex with her."

He nods at nothing. "We did it the night before we left for the cruise. That was the last time."

"If she's just finding out she's pregnant now, she must have gotten pregnant either at the very end of the cruise or maybe even after. I suppose it's theoretically possible she could have gotten pregnant from Ed if she slept with him immediately after she got back to Seattle after leaving the boat."

He snorts and looks away. "She must have been doing it with him before the cruise. Then she roped him into this whole fiancé thing so she could have another fish on the line as soon as the divorce goes through."

I can't stand the way his features pinch when he says it. I go over to him and put my arm around his back, but he barely notices that, either.

"I know it's weighing on your mind, but let's try to take your mind off it. Let's unload the car, make breakfast, and then get some sleep. This problem isn't going to go away from us stressing about it."

He jerks around and narrows his eyes at me. "This isn't my baby. You have to believe that. I never had anything to do with her after you told me she was screwing around with Carlos."

I have to smile up at him and then hug him. "Will you listen to yourself? This is the same thing we went through with Carlos except that it's on your side now. Of course it isn't your baby. Alexis is pulling the same nonsense on you that Carlos tried to pull on me. She's desperate, so she's throwing a Hail Mary in the last pathetic hope that she might be able to throw herself back on your hands. You don't have to worry about me. We're going to get through this the same way we got through Carlos's paternity suit."

He still looks so agitated and strained over this that I don't say anything else. The words bounce right off him.

He won't be able to relax until we get the results of the paternity test. No one has to explain that to me.

I wrap my arms around him and hug him. I don't expect him to respond, but his arms come to life, circle behind my back, and then he clasps my head and presses it into his chest.

"Thank you," he breathes. "Thank you for staying strong for me."

I lean back, cup both his cheeks, and stare deep into his eyes. "We're going to get through this. This is a temporary speed bump on the road. It will pass and become part of the past. As soon as we deal with this, we never have to deal with her or Carlos ever again. Now come on. We have more important things to think about. What are you hungry for—breakfast or lunch?"

We get busy building our new life together. We work together to unpack the car and I start making sandwiches for both of us. It's already late in the morning and our biological clocks are way off from driving all night.

I put the sandwiches on the plates, and when I look up, I spot Nate sitting on the couch. He's reading the paternity suit paperwork again.

So much for that. He'll be thinking about almost nothing else from now on.

I don't call him to eat at the table. I take his plate and a bottle of juice to the couch and put his food and drink on the coffee table.

He doesn't see it. I lean back, put my plate on my lap, and start eating. I don't say anything to him to interrupt his thoughts. I'm sure I'll find out more than I ever wanted to know about all of that sooner than I want to.

Chapter 26: Holly

Nate squints through the windshield of his car at the office building in front of us. I know that look.

"Right," he snarls. "Let's get this over with."

He kicks the driver's door open, storms around the car, yanks open the passenger door, and extends his hand to help me get out.

He's been storming around like a steamroller these past few days. He glares at everything, constantly compresses his lips at everything, and slams doors a lot as the tension mounts.

The strain comes to a breaking point today. We're about to find out the results of the paternity test. No matter what else happens today, we'll be walking out of this building knowing who the father of Alexis's baby is.

I already think I have a pretty good idea who it is. I don't envy Carlos getting stuck with Alexis for the rest of some poor child's life. Carlos has no idea what he's getting into.

I feel sorry for the child, though. I wish I could give the kid a decent life with a decent mother, but that's someone else's problem now.

Maybe having a child will be the wake-up call Alexis needs to pull her life together. I can only hope.

I have more to worry about from Nate. The stress he's under is really starting to show. I feel for the guy, but today will settle it once and for all.

At least he'll walk out of here with answers. We'll be able to move forward.

He keeps going over the sequence of events again and again. He gets obsessed with Alexis's fertility cycle, when he did it with her last, when she started up with Carlos, and when she found out that he gave her gonorrhea.

I try to be gentle with Nate and go over the dates with him. He needs to reassure himself that this isn't his baby.

I really don't see how this could be Carlos's baby, either. The numbers just don't add up. She couldn't have been fertile the last time she did it with Nate.

Then she tested positive for gonorrhea and had to wait a week before she got clearance from Dr. McKinlay that she could safely have sex with someone.

From what I can figure out, she wouldn't have become fertile until the middle of that week. Troy Nixon threw Carlos off the boat before Alexis could have sex with anyone else.

I drive myself crazy with all the intricate, complicated details. I try to push them out of my head and think about other things, but I have to be there to help Nate process everything.

He takes my hand on our way into the building, but his hand doesn't communicate the same warmth and connection it usually does. He's a million miles away.

He opens the lobby doors and escorts me to the elevators. He goes through the whole process mechanically like we aren't really together.

He barely sees me these last few days. He doesn't see anything but this problem looming in his face.

Some part of me almost wishes this was his baby. I could almost wish I could give that child the stabilizing influence the child will need in its life.

I could show the child what a real mother is supposed to look like. The child could have a normal life in those times when they come to stay with me and Nate before they have to go back to the chaos of living with Alexis.

That isn't going to happen because this isn't Nate's child. It's almost a shame, but I don't tell him that. I won't have to because this child will never come to stay with us.

We ride up to the twentieth floor and meet Nate's lawyer in another lobby. His lawyer is a middle-aged guy named Martin Engelman.

Martin takes excellent care of himself. He has broad shoulders, a broad powerful back, and strong, muscular hands. A thick, brown mustache covers his upper lip. He has a Josef Stalin kind of look with a determined, unbending air that instantly puts me at ease.

His crisp green eyes snap every time he looks at something. He compresses his lips when he sees me and Nate holding hands. I don't know what that means, but the world better get used to me and Nate being together.

"Don't say a single word in there," Martin growls under his breath. "Understand? Don't talk to the complainant. Don't talk to the other parties or the other lawyers. Don't say anything to anyone. Let me do all the talking on your behalf."

"I understand," Nate replies. "Don't worry. I don't want to talk to any of them."

"This should be over real quick as soon as we hear the results," Martin goes on. "Then you can leave."

Nate nods. "That's what I'm hoping."

Martin claps him on the shoulder. "We went over this already. It can't be yours and it isn't yours. Just get through this meeting and the nightmare will be over."

Nate nods again and Martin leads us into another conference room. Carlos is there with Pedro Alvarez. Alexis stands on the far side of the room with two men in suits.

One of them looks like a young business tycoon in an immaculately tailored black suit and polished black boots. He has almost white-blonde hair. His eyebrows and eyelashes are so pale that they're almost invisible.

The other guy looks like an IT tech at a mid-level computer repair company. He looks completely out of place here. That has to be Ed Conway, Alexis's new meal ticket.

Ed is also young—a lot younger than Alexis. He wears his sandy brown hair cut in a longish bowl style. I can't see from here what color his eyes are.

His suit doesn't fit him as well as it could. It almost looks like he picked it up at a garage sale. He stands with his hands in his pockets and looks around in confusion at everything.

I feel bad for the guy that Alexis's drama roped him into this. Ed keeps fidgeting and adjusting his shoulders inside his jacket.

Alexis pours on the charm with her elegant lawyer. She smiles at him in a way she doesn't smile at Ed. The poor guy is just a vehicle for her. He's a pit stop on the way to her next conquest.

Her lawyer is the one who calls the meeting together, invites everyone to sit down at the table, and introduces himself as Roark Brighton.

He, Alexis, and Ed arrange themselves at the head of the table. The rest of us sit farther down with me, Nate, and Martin on one side and Carlos and Pedro on the other.

"Let's get straight to the matter, shall we?" Roark announces. "You've all received sealed copies of the paternity results. We'll unseal them at the same time and share the results with each other. Then we can determine the rights and responsibilities for the man who turns out to be a positive match as the father of this child."

Martin and Pedro both agree. The three lawyers take out their envelopes and tear them open.

Martin reads his and hands the paperwork to Nate. I bend over to read the results.

The results include multiple pages stapled together. Each sheet lists the DNA results for one man tested against the amnio sample taken from Alexis's uterus.

The top sheet gives the results for Nate. The highlighted results say there is a zero percent chance he could be the father.

He takes one look at the number and flips to the next page. This one lists the results for Carlos Silverman. The results say there is a zero percent chance he could be the father of the baby, too.

Nate turns to the last page. This page gives the results for Ed Conway. I'm not even surprised when the results say he has a zero percent chance of being this child's father, too.

Nate shoots me a wild smirk and immediately wipes his face of all expression when he hands the results back to Martin.

Martin, Pedro, and Roark pass their sheets around so everyone can confirm that they all got the same results.

"This is outrageous!" Alexis huffs. "I want to challenge the results."

"What does this mean?" Ed stammers. "I don't understand."

"It means you aren't the father of this baby," Roark tells him with saint-like patience. "It means neither Mr. Silverman nor Mr. Whitman are the father of this baby, either. None of you are."

"But how can I not be?" Ed asks. "We're engaged."

"This is my child!" Carlos blurts out. "You came between us! You pushed us away from each other!"

I can't believe it when Carlos starts yelling at Ed across the table.

Ed looks around at him in confusion and even fear. "I don't even know you, man! I never even knew you were with her."

"He wasn't," Roark interrupts by holding out his hand to Ed. "Don't listen to him. He wasn't with her after she came back from the cruise."

"Then how is this not my baby?" Ed's eyes dart everywhere. "I don't understand."

"That depends on how active Ms. Whitman was between the last time she slept with Mr. Silverman and when she got together with you." Roark casts a sidelong glance at Alexis. "Why don't you ask her? I'm sure she can tell you."

Alexis squirms in her chair. She also looks around, but she doesn't make eye contact with anyone. Dang! That has to sting.

She cowers and hunches her shoulders the way she did when Troy busted her in the bar trying to hook up with guys while she was still contagious.

Ed turns to her. His expression changes from confusion to unimaginable sadness. Does he finally get it now?

His voice quakes. "Baby? What's going on here? Why didn't you tell me? You said you loved me."

Nate's hand flies to mine under the table. He clasps it in a warm, comforting squeeze. Thank all the stars in Heaven I'm going home with him today.

"How could you do this to me?" Ed's voice starts to rise. "You said we were going to be a family together."

"Why don't you ask her how many men she slept with on the cruise?" Roark interrupts. "Ask her how many men she engaged in sexual contact with after Mr. Silverman left the ship."

Ouch. Alexis's own lawyer is turning against her—or maybe he's Ed's lawyer. That makes more sense.

"Baby?" Ed asks. "Answer me. How many guys did you hook up with on the cruise?"

"It wasn't like that!" Alexis waves him away. "You know what cruises are like. People like to let their hair down."

"Just give us the number," Roark insists. "One of them is the father of this child, so we'll need to track him down—unless it's someone you got together with after you came back from the cruise."

"That's impossible," Ed interjects. "We've been together since she came back from the cruise."

"Unless she cheated on you the same way she cheated on her husband and me and everyone else," Carlos cuts in. "Wake up, dude. You didn't really think you were the only one, did you? She did it to everyone else. She'll do it to you, too."

Ed stares at him and then turns back to stare at Alexis. His expression finally changes to cold, distant, disgust when he puts the pieces together.

She either slept with everyone who was willing on the cruise or she kept sleeping around even after she came back and maneuvered Ed into taking her under his wing.

His voice goes deadly still. It doesn't shake or break anymore. "How many?" he murmurs. "How many men did you sleep with on the cruise?"

"I don't know, okay?!" she blurts out. "I didn't count them!"

He raises his eyebrows. "You slept with more men than you can count—on a two-week cruise? What did you do—advertise?"

"It wasn't like that!" she insists, but Roark interrupts what could turn out to be an ugly scene.

"We'll need to get the full list of names so we can alert them to this paternity filing," Rourke announces.

"I don't know their names!" Alexis snaps back.

Ed flinches and turns his head away. He definitely gets it now.

Martin saves the day by standing up. "Well, this business no longer concerns my client. We'll just bid you gentlemen good day and you can take it from here without us."

He shakes hands with Roark and Pedro, nods to Carlos, Alexis, and Ed, and Martin steers me and Nate out of the room.

Martin puffs out his cheeks in the upstairs lobby as soon as we get outside. "Phew! I don't envy the lady. I really don't."

"Wow," Nate breathes. "This is so much worse than I thought it would be. That poor kid."

Martin makes a face at him. "We really should require an entrance exam and integrity test before people are allowed to become parents." He shakes himself. "Never mind. You're in the clear. You can go home and forget about all of this."

"Thank you, man." Nate holds out his hand to shake Martin's. "I can't thank you enough."

"Thank *you,*" Martin exclaims. "Thank you for being a solid individual and not turning my representation of you into a Jerry-Springer circus farce."

Nate laughs in relief for the first time. "Thank you for not taking me out of the room too soon. I really needed to see that for myself."

Martin smirks and then breaks out in laughter. "I thought you might." He claps Nate on the shoulder again. "You escaped. Go home and start living your life. You deserve it."

Martin shakes hands with me and leaves. Nate turns to me and clasps my hand. His eyes overflow with so much painful relief and heartfelt gratitude.

"I can't thank you enough for being there for me through all of this," he murmurs. "You never let me down. I'm sorry I've been on edge lately."

"Stop," I tell him. "You had every right to be and you also had every right to my support." I squeeze his hand. "Let's go home. We have way too much to do. Hey! We're having a baby, remember?"

He smiles, but his features spasm with buried emotion. "Yeah. I remember."

I rise on my tiptoes to put my arms around his neck to hug him, but he doesn't let it turn into a quick, comforting hug.

He closes his arms around my back and pulls me into a deep, powerful hug that doesn't end. He holds me close and buries his face in my hair. "You're everything good about my life. I don't know what I did to get lucky enough to get you, but I'm so grateful to have you."

I shut my eyes and my hand flies to the back of his head. I hug him back feeling this overwhelming gratitude that my life turned out the way it is.

He's everything I ever wanted Carlos to be—and so much more. I didn't realize there was anything wrong with my marriage to Carlos, but I must have always known in the bottommost corner of my gut.

I didn't realize it until I got together with Nate. Now this overwhelming sense of rightness steers everything we do. Everything about this fits together in ways I never thought possible.

The love between us radiates between our bodies. It forms a nucleus of energy and potential that grows inside me right now.

That energy will blossom into another human being. The love between us will become a three-way street as soon as another little person joins our lives. Then more people will join us to become a family—our family.

I feel all of that when I hold Nate in my arms. It all starts right here.

I don't want to stop holding him and feeling this, but we have to break apart eventually. That energy and potential glows between us even when we let go of each other and straighten up to look into each other's eyes.

I don't want to lose that feeling, either. I want to keep looking until I don't see anything else, but I have to.

He bursts into a glorious smile of pure happiness and his eyes brim with glistening emotion when he squeezes both my hands.

He can barely get his voice to make any sound when he husks, "Let's go home."

End of Book 2.

Keep Reading

P<u>aradise Cruises Series: Book 2: Missing Persons</u>

Jenn Hayworth thought she was coming on the cruise of a lifetime when she and her boyfriend Donovan McNulty board theParadise Cruise ship *Electric Emerald*. All those romantic dreams come crashing down around their ears when Donovan catches Jenn staring at another man. Donovan doesn't believe her when she tells him the guy looks identical to her cousin who disappeared overseas five years ago.

She has to find out if this stranger is her missing cousin—but will getting the answers she needs cost her relationship? Is it worth it?

Marco De Rossi can't believe his eyes when he sees a woman on board the *Electric Emerald* who exactly resembles his missing sister Becca. His girlfriend Angeline Harvey goes ballistic that he's getting interested in another woman. Angeline forbids Marco even to speak to the woman—not even to find out if she is his missing sister.

The darkest secrets of the past are lurking just beneath the surface and waiting to tear these lives apart when worlds collide and the truth comes out. No one will be prepared for the avalanche of consequences or what this could mean to the two couples' future.

You can find it at your favorite book retailer.

Sign Up Once--Get all A.E. Moran's free books including brand new releases

The Paradise Cruise ship *Electric Emerald* is buzzing with the news that Stella Lowell is getting married in two days on board the ship. Stella's family, her fiancé Beau, and Beau's family are all on board and over-the-top excited for the big day.

Too bad Stella isn't over-the-top excited for the big day—or for her fiancé and soon to be husband.

The whole catastrophe blows up when Stella's brother Silas interferes with her talking to a man at the bar. It turns out Silas knows Walker Shockley from their time at school together—and Silas has nothing good to say about Walker.

The disastrous results will be far worse than just a wedding nightmare beyond anyone's worst fears. Nothing is what it seems—and no one is what they seem, either. Life has a way of interfering in the best laid plans. Will the result be the life of Stella's dreams or the worst thing that could ever happen to her?

Sign up at www.authoraemoran.com to read it for free.

About AE Moran

A .E Moran is the contemporary romance pen name for Theo Mann.

I write 70 books per year—and yes, before you ask, all these books are my original creative work. Nothing written under my name is AI-generated or ghostwritten because I write better than AI and any ghostwriter out there.

People don't read fiction for entertainment or to escape from reality. People read fiction to see their humanity reflected in another person's character and story.

This is my promise to you. When you read my books, you'll see your own humanity reflected in the characters and stories. I take this commitment to my readers very seriously. My books are an intimate form of communication between us. I would never disrespect my readers by turning that over to a machine or another writer. This is my bond between me and you as my reader.

I write 20,000 words per day as my daily work output. If anyone with a public platform would like to challenge me to prove this in a controlled environment, feel free to contact me on this website's contact page. How do I do write so much? Find out more on my blog, *Crimes Against Fiction* at www.theomann.com.

I worked as a professional ghostwriter for fifteen years. Now I'm going for the Guinness World Record by writing 700 books over the next ten years and 1400 books over the next twenty years, all originally written by me.

See my website for the full book list. I'm also the author of *Proof for the Existence of God* and the *Crimes Against Fiction* blog.

You can find out more at www.theomann.com or at www.author aemoran.com.

Also by AE Moran (so far)